THE LAST HOLIDAY CONCERT

THE LAST
HOLIDAY
CONCERT

Andrew Clements

SCHOLASTIC INC.

> *For my sons,*
> *George William Clements and Charles Philip Clements*

A special thanks to these dedicated music teachers: Richard Hagar, Cynthia Hamburger, David Jost, Vickie Livermore, Marjorie Olson, William Pappazisis, David Seaman, Joseph Stillitano, and Paul Tomashefsky.

No part of this publication may be reproduced, stored in a retrieval system, or transmitted in any form or by any means, electronic, mechanical, photocopying, recording, or otherwise, without written permission of the publisher. For information regarding permission, write to Atheneum Books for Young Readers, an imprint of Simon & Schuster Children's Publishing Division, 1230 Avenue of the Americas, New York, NY 10020.

ISBN 978-0-545-59812-5

12 11 10 9 8 7 6   14 15 16 17 18/0

Printed in the U.S.A.   40

First Scholastic printing, November 2013

Book design by Greg Stadnyk
The text for this book is set in Revival.

"Let There Be Peace on Earth" by Jill Jackson and Sy Miller.
Copyright © 1955 by Jan-Lee Music. Copyright renewed 1983.
All rights reserved. Reprinted by permission of Jan-Lee Music. Grateful acknowledgment to Santorella Publications, Ltd. of Danvers, MA 01923, for the use of the sheet music arrangement of "Let There Be Peace on Earth."

One

PALMER KIDS

Hart Evans sat in the front row at the second big assembly of the year. The kids from the last few homerooms hadn't found their seats yet, so there was plenty of noise. Hart turned and looked around the auditorium, sweeping his eyes from left to right. There were still a lot of unfamiliar faces in the crowd, even after two and a half months of school.

Then, as the last group of kids sat down, Hart saw something he had never noticed before. What Hart saw was the complete sixth grade, almost four hundred students. The thought that came to him was like a vision, a burst of understanding.

And Hart said to himself, *We're the Palmer kids now!*

In the town of Brentbury, kids went to kindergarten, first, second, third, fourth, and fifth grades at Collins Elementary School or at Newman Elementary School. Like two streams tumbling down different sides of the same hill, the Collins kids and the Newman kids bubbled along separately for six years. Those two streams of children flowed together for the first time at Palmer Intermediate, where they became a swirling pool of sixth graders. Palmer Intermediate School contained the sixth grade, the whole sixth grade, and nothing but the sixth grade.

Every fall it took a couple months for the new sixth graders to stop thinking of themselves as Newman kids or Collins kids. By October or November it began to sink in: *We're the Palmer kids now.*

So Hart was right on time.

Hart Evans liked being at Palmer Intermediate. It was so different from elementary school. Part of that had to do with the building. Everything was bigger—bigger gym, bigger cafeteria, bigger playing fields, and a big auditorium with a full stage. Until about fifteen years ago Palmer had been the junior high school, and that's what it felt like.

That's also how Palmer School was run, like a junior high. All the kids had lockers. They had homeroom in the morning, and then moved from class to class, subject to subject, teacher to teacher for the rest of the day. It was a whole new school experience. Making the jump to Palmer Intermediate made Hart feel like he was finally getting somewhere.

One of Hart's favorite things about Palmer School was that his little sister Sarah was somewhere else. She was in fourth grade now, two years behind him back at Collins Elementary. Since her first day of kindergarten, Sarah had been like a piece of gum stuck to the bottom of Hart's shoe. She had never missed a chance to tease or bother or embarrass her big brother. Plus Sarah was nosy, and a huge tattletale. And she had never ever accepted the fact that Hart was the most popular boy at Collins Elementary School, which was true.

Sarah didn't understand why everybody liked her brother so much. But clearly, they did. Who always had fifteen guys crowding around his table at lunch? Hart. Who got picked first at recess for baseball or dodgeball, even though he wasn't the best player? Hart. And who got invited to everybody's birthday party—at least two invitations each week—all year long? Same guy: Hart.

Sarah knew a different side of Hart Evans. At school he was Mr. Cool. At home, he was more like a nerd, or maybe a mad scientist. Hart even had his own workbench, which was really just an old corner desk. It had four skinny legs and one wide drawer that ran across the longest side of the triangular top. He'd spotted the desk at the end of someone's driveway one Saturday morning on the way back from soccer.

"Mom, quick! Stop the car! I need that desk. It's perfect!"

"Honey, that's just junk. You already have a nice desk."

"But that one's for schoolwork, Mom. I need a place where I can make things and mess around—you know, like for science projects. It'll fit right into the corner back by my closet. You won't even know it's there."

But his sister Sarah knew it was there. When Hart wasn't home she would snoop around to see what kind of goofy stuff he was up to. Like using the electric drill he'd gotten last Christmas to make tiny holes in pennies and bottle caps and acorns and pencils, and just about everything else. Like using glue to make sculptures out of nails and chunks of rock and rusty nuts and bolts. Like making huge fake boogers out of dried rubber cement, or using bits of blue and green bottle glass to make weird little stained glass windows. And how had Hart melted all those plastic milk jugs into that big lumpy mess, and why did he have so many different kinds of rubber bands—bags and bags of them?

Ever since nursery school Sarah had been trailing along two years behind her brother, and her identity was always discovered. "Your last name is Evans, right?" That was usually the first question. Then Sarah would see the teacher size her up and slowly put it all together—the shape of her face, her blue eyes and sandy brown hair, her slim build and slightly above average height, just like her brother's. And then the teacher would get this cheery look on her face and say, "Ohhh, yes—you must be *Hart*'s little sister, right?" And Sarah would nod and smile. By second grade she had stopped smiling. And in third grade Sarah had said, "Yes, Hart is my fantastic, wonderful, glorious older brother, and I would appreciate it if no one mentions his name again. Ever."

Sarah's friends would say, "Hart Evans is your *brother*? He's so *cool*!" And Sarah had to explain that, based on *her* observations, Hart was actually a total dweeb.

But all that was in Hart's past. Sarah didn't even ride the same bus with him anymore. At Palmer Intermediate School Hart was on his own.

Palmer kids. Looking around at all the sixth graders, Hart wrestled with the idea. He couldn't put it into words, but he got a strange feeling—like he was looking at himself in the rearview mirror of a time machine. He saw that these four hundred kids were going to travel into the future with him. These were the kids he'd be on teams with in junior high and high school. They'd go to football games and dances together. They would get their driver's licenses and go hang out at Peak's Diner. These were the kids he would graduate from high school with, these Palmer kids. He was looking at his *class*, really looking at it for the first time.

Then Hart Evans, the visionary seer of the future, remembered the tangled wad of rubber bands in his pocket, and in a split second he was a sixth grade kid again.

Not that Hart had immediate plans to launch a rubber band. No way. Not during an assembly. And certainly not from the front row—much too dangerous. Hart hadn't been caught shooting a rubber band in over two years, and he planned to keep it that way.

No, the rubber bands in his pocket were for later, after lunch. Because after lunch it would be time for chorus. And in Hart's opinion, a few well-launched rubber bands were just what the sixth grade chorus needed.

Two

COOLNESS

Hart swallowed a yawn, but it was a tired yawn, not a bored yawn. He liked assemblies. Sometimes the programs were good, and even if they weren't, an assembly was still pretty much free time. As long as you kept looking straight ahead and didn't shut your eyes, you could think about anything you wanted to for almost an hour—which didn't happen very often at school.

Up on stage two men and two women were dressed in costumes from the 1840s. The guy in the straw hat had a banjo, and the woman wearing blue-jean overalls had a guitar. All four were singing some songs about the Erie Canal. They were good musicians, and the way they used folk songs to show American history was pretty interesting. But they'd been at it for almost thirty-five minutes and it was starting to get old. Hart tuned them out.

Another yawn.

Hart let his mind drift back a few hours, and he remembered the sound of the noisy water pipes in the wall next to his bed, which was why he'd been awake since six AM today. That was when his dad had started taking a shower. Hart had tried to get back to sleep, but the automatic coffeemaker had already filled the house with the smell of morning.

Usually his mom had to pull Hart out of bed at the last second so he could throw on some clothes, drag a comb through his hair, grab a piece of toast and a swallow of juice, and then sprint to catch the school bus. And as he hurried through the kitchen Sarah always said something like, "It's so *stupid* to be late!"

Not today. Hart was starting a second bowl of cereal when his parents had come into the kitchen a little before seven.

His mom had been surprised. "Are you feeling all right, Hartie?"

And Hart had said, "I'm fine, Mom. I just woke up early, that's all. And please—stop calling me Hartie, okay?"

"Fifteen years on the Erie Canal!"

Up onstage the two men came out wearing a

mule costume and began towing a barge around. Hart smiled, but he kept thinking about the morning.

It had only taken his dad about three minutes to get ready, scanning the front page of the morning paper while he poured coffee into his travel mug. Then Mom had handed him a toasted bagel wrapped in a napkin, got a kiss in return, and Dad was all set to go.

That's when Hart had popped the question: "Dad, can you drive me to school today?"

"Sorry, Hart. I've got to beat the traffic, and if I drove you now, you'd be there almost an hour early."

After the front door closed, Hart had listened for the rumble as his dad started the new sports car. He'd only had it about three weeks.

"Low bridge, everybody down!"

The performers were trying to get the sixth graders to sing along on the chorus of the song. It wasn't working.

Hart thought, *No wonder Dad gets up early and drives to the city every morning—with a car that sweet, who wouldn't?*

Hart couldn't wait to get dropped off at school in that car. He could see it. His dad would turn into the wide front circle, whip past the parked buses, and come to a crisp stop at the front walk. The door of the silver roadster would swing open, and as all the kids turned to stare, Hart would step out. He'd slam the door, wave to his dad, and then the little bullet car would blaze off down Highway 12.

That hadn't happened, not yet.

But it wasn't like Hart actually needed any help in the coolness department. Hart Evans was well on his way to becoming the most popular boy at Palmer Intermediate, just like he had been for the last two years at Collins Elementary School. It had never been a contest. Plenty of guys at school were more handsome. A lot of guys were tougher, and some were smarter, too. Didn't matter. Hart was still the coolest. Even his name was cool: Hart, which was short for Hartford—also a cool name.

Zack Banks and Alex Neely were Hart's two best friends at Palmer Intermediate. Alex was a little taller than Hart, but not at all athletic.

He loved to read, and he had a quick mind and a sharp sense of humor. He lived near Hart, and they'd gone to Collins Elementary together. Hart called Alex whenever he had a computer issue, or whenever he didn't understand an assignment, or anytime he needed a good laugh. And they still sat together on the bus every morning, just as they had all through grade school. One of their strongest common interests was in the junk collecting department. The trash pickup in Brentbury was early Wednesday morning, and when the weather was right, Hart and Alex rode their bikes around for a Tuesday night treasure hunt.

Alex understood that Hart was popular, but he wasn't impressed—except by the way girls talked to Hart. Right before the Halloween dance Alex had said, "I give you permission to put in a good word about me to Regina. Or maybe Emily. Or Caroline. Or Sue. Or any girl. Please."

Zack was a different story. Zack had dark curly hair and a big smile, and he was the best soccer player in Brentbury's junior league. He was plenty popular on his own, but during the first week of sixth grade Zack had looked around and decided that being friends with Hart would be a smart move. They were in the same homeroom, so it had been pretty easy.

"You and me, Hart," Zack said one day with a wink, "we've got it made." And there was some truth to that, and Hart knew it. The difference was that Hart didn't work at being popular. It came naturally.

Just this morning, milling around in the crowd outside the auditorium, at least a dozen different kids had smiled or waved at Hart, trying to catch his eye, hoping for something in return. Because if Hart noticed you, it made you feel good. And Hart was generous. He nodded at Lee, and smiled at Steve, and he said, "Hey, Tommy." And then came a nod to a guy on the other side of the hall, and then "Dan—how's it goin'? Great shoes—those new?" And it wasn't a fakey nice. Hart was for real.

No one was immune to Hart's good nature, his easy self-confidence. When he apologized as he turned in his first social studies report a day late, Mrs. Moughty had said, "I'm still going to have to lower your grade, Hart." But she didn't.

When Hart got caught swinging on the rope in the gym, Mr. Harvis shouted, "Evans, that'll be ten laps—after school!" Then, when a smiling Hart Evans showed up at three o'clock sharp, the gym teacher growled, "Go on, catch your bus—but don't let it happen again." Hart could have charmed the hairnet off a cafeteria lady.

It was almost Thanksgiving, but to Hart, it felt like the school year was practically over. The days flipped by, and sixth grade at Palmer Intermediate was turning out to be a breeze. His friends were good, his classes were only a minor disruption in his busy social life, and the homework wasn't too bad either. In short, school was great. Hart felt like he owned the place.

Except, that is, on Monday, Tuesday, Wednesday, Thursday, and Friday, right after lunch. Because that was when it was time for chorus. And for Mr. Meinert.

Hart actually loved music. He had taken two years of piano lessons, and recently he'd also begun to play a band instrument—the coolest one, of course—the drums. Except the sixth grade band already had three other more experienced drummers. And that was why Hart had been put into the chorus.

He even had a decent singing voice—at least, it sounded good to him when he sang in the shower. So music itself wasn't the problem. Hart just didn't like chorus.

He didn't like standing up and opening his mouth wide and singing songs that he never would have chosen to sing on his own. Hart liked *his* music and *his* songs, and he liked to sing them *his* way. Not Mr. Meinert's way.

And then there were the concerts. They were the worst part of the whole deal. The school year seemed like an endless flow of programs and performances—first it was the "Halloween Spooker," and then came the holiday concert, and then the "Midwinter Sing-Along," then the "Spring-Has-Sprung" program, and finally, finally, the "Graduation Celebration."

Concerts meant learning new songs, and that meant singing them over and over again.

And then there was the whole rigamarole of standing up and sitting down together, and walking on and off the stage, and not fidgeting on the risers, and holding the little folder of sheet music, and wearing the white shirt and the black pants and the black socks and the black shoes.

Hart was sure that Mr. Meinert had designed the entire chorus experience so it would be as awkward and annoying and uncomfortable as humanly possible. Chorus simply was not cool, not one bit of it, which meant that chorus cramped Hart's style in the worst possible way.

Because at one end of the Palmer School universe there was Hart and his slowly rotating galaxy of ultimate coolness. Then way, way down at the other end of time and space, past all the stars and moons and planets, there was Mr. Meinert, singing his head off somewhere inside a very uncool black hole.

Since it was almost Thanksgiving Mr. Meinert was already doing the big push to get ready for the holiday concert. And it was a push. A one-hour musical extravaganza required a massive effort, and from Mr. Meinert's point of view, *his* chorus was the main event of the whole show. For over a week Mr. Meinert hadn't even tried to tell any jokes. He'd been stiff and grumpy and more demanding than ever.

"Just to pass the time away . . ."

The last song of the morning assembly was "I've Been Working on the Railroad," and the performers asked all the kids to stand up and sing along. The banjo player kept stopping the song to shout, "Can't you kids sing louder than *that?*" By the third time he'd done it, they were all screaming the words at the tops of their lungs, and when the song ended, the applause was so loud and went on so long that Mr. Richards the principal had to get up on the stage and make everyone be quiet.

As the kids began leaving the auditorium, Hart caught a glimpse of Mr. Meinert at the side of the stage, thanking the performers.

Hart smiled, and he thought, *See you after lunch, Mr. Meinert.*

Today, for the first time all year, Hart was pretty sure that chorus was going to be fun.

Three

MISFIRE

Hart knew he was taking a risk. He didn't care. By his calculation, chorus was ten times more annoying than anything else at school—which was saying a lot. Hart felt like chorus needed some excitement—and the risk? Well, that was part of the fun.

The sixth grade chorus was trying to learn "Up on the Housetop." Each boy and girl stood in front of a folding desk, and each of them held an old songbook. The music room was shaped like a half circle, and the four stair-stepped levels made it look like the kids were standing on risers.

The altos kept murdering their harmony part, so Mr. Meinert was making everyone sing the first verse and the refrain again and again and again. Standing down at the front of the room behind an electric piano, he played the melody with his right hand, swung his left arm through the air to keep the rhythm, and sang out the alto part at the top of his lungs, trying to pound the notes into the heads of about thirty sixth-grade girls. He kept having to push his dark hair up off his forehead. His brown eyes flashed warning after warning, and his face got redder and redder. Anyone could see that Mr. Meinert was in no mood for messing around.

Hart had chosen the classic Number 16 rubber band for today's raid. Before stretching, a Number 16 rubber band measures 1/16 of an inch thick and 2 1/2 inches from end to end. It has an effective range of about twenty feet. In the hands of an expert, a Number 16 is almost silent and remarkably accurate.

Hart stood at the left side of the room with most of the other boys. His voice was pretty deep, so he wasn't up in the front row, and that was good. Keeping his eyes on Mr. Meinert, Hart pulled a fresh Number 16 out of his front pocket. He looped one end around the top corner of the stiff cover of his music book. He stretched the rubber band back about four inches, and then pressed it against the edge of the book with his index finger.

He was loaded and ready.

Hart raised the music book and shifted his weight so he had a clear launch path between Jimmy Lohman and Bill Ralston. He felt his hands begin to sweat. As they sang *"Ho, ho, ho, who wouldn't go?"* Mr. Meinert turned to face the girls, just as he had before. And Hart lifted his finger.

The rubber band zipped past Jimmy's right ear, traced a graceful arc in front of the rolling blackboard, bounced once on Mr. Meinert's slanted music stand, and then stuck on the front of his sweater—a little tan circle on the dark green wool.

Mr. Meinert didn't notice it. He did notice a flutter of giggles in the room, but he stopped them with a shake of his head. The song went on.

Hart should have stopped while he was ahead. But he didn't. He pulled out a fresh rubber band and before he loaded it onto the edge of the music book, Hart twisted it into a double loop to give it extra force. He was going to put this one up into the fluorescent lights above Mr. Meinert's head. He pulled back the doubled rubber band, adjusted his aim, and at the next *"Up on the housetop, click, click, click,"* Hart released shot number two.

Maybe his finger slipped. Maybe Hart had stretched the band too far. Or maybe he shouldn't have used the double loop. Because the rubber band flew straight and fast and hard, and it snapped smack into the side of Mr. Meinert's neck.

The piano stopped as Mr. Meinert jerked his head like he'd been stung by a bee. He slapped at his neck and ducked his head, looking around quickly to try to spot a hornet or a wasp. Some of the kids laughed, and Mr. Meinert knew he must have looked silly. He smiled and held his hands up to quiet everyone down. He said, "Okay, show's over. Let's take it from the beginning of the refrain again."

He looked down at his piano, and that's when he saw the rubber bands—one on the keyboard, and the other hanging on his sweater.

Mr. Meinert's eyes narrowed. His lips twitched and slowly twisted into an angry frown. There was a hushed moment of calm, and then the storm.

"WHO?" he boomed. "WHO DID THIS?" Eyes flashing, he snatched up the rubber bands. Pinching them between his thumb and forefinger, he shook them out in front of his face.

"WHO?" he shouted again. "Who shot these?" He stalked out from behind his piano. "Who? Tell me *right now*!"

A man who gets hopping mad, who gets so angry that he sputters and spits and stomps around, all red in the face with his eyes bugging out and his teeth showing—in a comedy movie or a TV show, that can be very funny. In real life, it's not.

Realizing that the shots must have come from his right, Mr. Meinert spun to face the boys. "NOW!" he bellowed. "Tell me now! Who did this?" Mr. Meinert looked quickly from face to face, and when he locked eyes with Hart, he knew.

"*You!*" He pointed at Hart's face. "It was you, right? RIGHT? *Answer me*!"

Hart couldn't think. He'd never seen a teacher this angry before. All his coolness melted. Hart gave a guilty little nod.

In a flash Mr. Meinert had hold of Hart's

arm, steering him toward the door. They were out of the room and down the hall to the office in fifteen seconds. The man walked so fast Hart had to trot to keep from being dragged along. Breathing hard, Mr. Meinert's face was still twisted with anger. Through clenched teeth he kept saying, "Very *funny! Very funny*!"

The door to the principal's office was closed, and Mr. Meinert knocked and pushed it open in one move. Mr. Richards looked up from the papers on his desk as Mr. Meinert shouted, "This . . . this young man thought it would be *funny* to shoot me in the neck with a rubber band!"

The principal looked from Mr. Meinert's bright red face to Hart's pale one.

He nodded at Mr. Meinert and said, "You can let go of his arm. He's not going to run away."

Mr. Meinert dropped Hart's arm. Then he held up a rubber band and said, "This is the one that hit me in the neck."

Mr. Richards looked at Hart. "Is that right, Hart? Did you shoot that rubber band?"

Hart gulped and found his voice. "I . . . I did

shoot it, but I wasn't aiming it at him. Honest. And I'm sorry. I was aiming way above him, at the lights. Really."

"Oh, *sure*!" said Mr. Meinert, shouting again. "And it just *happens* to hit me right in the neck." Holding up the other rubber band, he said, "And what about *this* one, the one that stuck on my sweater? I suppose you were aiming *this* one at the lights too?"

The principal stood up. "Mr. Meinert, please. There's no need to shout. I'd like you to go back to your classroom now. Is anyone there supervising the children?"

"Well, no," said Mr. Meinert, "but . . . but this was . . . it was an *attack*. It was an emergency."

Mr. Richards nodded. "I understand what you're saying, and we'll get it all sorted out. But you need to get back to your classroom. I'll deal with Hart."

Mr. Meinert turned, gave Hart a last angry look, and stomped out of the office.

Mr. Richards sat back down in his chair. Hart looked across the desk at him. "Really, I didn't mean to hit him. And that first shot? I aimed it at his music stand, and then the rubber band bounced onto his sweater. It just bounced. That's the way it happened, I swear. I wasn't trying to hit anybody."

Mr. Richards looked at Hart a long moment and then said, "I believe you—that hitting him was an accident. But there's no excuse for shooting rubber bands in the first place. If that rubber band had hit Mr. Meinert in the eye, we'd be looking at a big problem here. Do you have any more?"

Hart dug into his pocket and then dumped the rubber bands onto the desk.

"How about in your locker?"

Hart shook his head. "No, that's all I have."

Mr. Richards said, "I'm keeping you after school today. And tomorrow. Come here to the office, and I expect you to bring homework or a book to read. Is that clear?"

Hart nodded. Then he said, "Um . . . can I call my mom? She doesn't get home until a half hour after I do, and she doesn't like my little sister to be alone after school."

Mr. Richards glanced at his watch. "Hmm . . . I see. In that case, you can serve your detentions starting tomorrow. Tell your parents that you'll be staying after school for one hour both tomorrow and Friday. And tell them why. And no more rubber bands at school. Understood?"

Hart nodded. Then he said, "So . . . so I can go now?"

Mr. Richards nodded. "Yes, you may go."

Hart left the principal's office, but as he reached the door to the hallway, Mr. Richards called, "Wait a second, Hart." Hart stopped and turned back.

Mr. Richards said, "Did you leave any belongings in the music room?"

Hart shook his head. "No. My book bag's in my locker."

Mr. Richards pointed at the long bench against the wall of the main office. "Then I want you to sit right there until this period is over."

Hart said, "Okay," and he walked over and sat down.

After Mr. Richards shut his door, Hart turned and looked up over his shoulder until he could see the clock above him. It was one forty-four. That meant he had nine minutes to wait. And think.

At first all Hart could think about was the crazed, angry look on Mr. Meinert's face. The guy had totally flipped out. Considering everything, Hart felt like he'd gotten off easy. And he felt like Mr. Richards was a pretty good guy. He felt like the principal had saved him from Mr. Meinert.

The principal was smart, too. Because Hart understood why the man had told him to wait in the office until the period was over. Mr. Richards didn't think it would be a good idea for Hart and Mr. Meinert to be in the same room again, at least not right away.

And Hart agreed. Completely.

Four

BAD BEHAVIOR

At seven minutes after three Mr. Meinert stormed into the principal's office.

"Please, *please* tell me I didn't just see that Evans kid getting on a bus to go home, out there laughing and joking around with all his buddies. Tell me I'm seeing things—like a kid who shoots a teacher with a rubber band going home instead of staying after school! Tell me I'm blind. Tell me I'm crazy. Tell me *something*, anything!"

Mr. Richards got up and closed his door. "David, this is the second time today I've had to ask you not to shout in my office. Please, sit down."

"I don't want to sit down!"

Mr. Richards glared at him. He pointed at one of the blue plastic chairs in front of his desk. "David, sit."

The principal sat in the other blue chair. "Yes, that was Hart, and you saw him getting on that bus because both his parents work, and his mom expects him to be at home with his younger sister after school. It would have been difficult for the parents if Hart had stayed for detention today. If a boy misbehaves, we punish the boy, not his parents. So relax. Starting tomorrow Hart will be staying after school for the next two days."

Mr. Meinert popped up halfway out of his chair. "Two days!? *Only two days?*"

Mr. Richards nodded. "That's right, two days detention. I don't believe Hart hit you on purpose, and he's staying after school two days for shooting rubber bands at school. That's fair, and that's the end of it. So let it go, David. Do you understand me? Let it go."

"Or what?" asked Mr. Meinert. "You can't fire me twice."

Mr. Richards paused. He'd had a feeling this was going to come up. In a gentler voice he said, "You haven't been fired, David, and you know it. It's a town budget crisis. All the schools are cutting staff. I told you that a month ago. And I had nothing to do with deciding that the art and music teachers would be the first ones to go. I know that losing your job is upsetting, but you cannot let your personal situation affect your behavior at school."

"*My* behavior!" Mr. Meinert made it all the way to his feet on that one. "What do you mean, *my* behavior?"

"David, sit down. I'm talking about this afternoon, with Hart. You overreacted. And I had to ask you to let go of the boy's arm. Do you have any idea how big a problem that could have been? . . . for you *and* for this school district? What if you had made bruises on Hart's arm? What if you had hurt his shoulder? That could have been on the evening news today—and for all we know, it still might be. The kind of anger you displayed today was completely unprofessional. So *that's* the behavior I'm talking about."

Mr. Meinert turned and looked out the windows. The last two buses were pulling away.

The principal kept talking. "I'm sorry about the town's money problems, and I'm very sorry your job will end on January first. You have a right to be upset about that—it's a rotten Christmas present. You're a terrific music teacher, David, and I hate losing you. But there's nothing I can do about it. I did get the school board to keep your names out of the local news until the Christmas vacation begins, and I understand why you and the other teachers made that request. It'd be even worse with everyone walking around feeling sorry for you. So . . . we all just have to make the best of a bad situation."

"Make the best of it," said Mr. Meinert, still facing the windows. "Easy for you to say."

"No," said Mr. Richards, "it's *not* easy. We went through this eight years ago, the same thing. And there's nothing easy about it—not for me, not for anyone." Mr. Meinert didn't respond, so the principal added, "If there were anything I could do about this, I'd have done it by now. I'm still hoping the district can come up with the money we need before the end of the year, but that's a long shot. And if I can help with recommendations as you look for other jobs, you know I've got nothing but good things to say about you and your work."

Mr. Meinert just sat there, his face turned away.

After an awkward silence, Mr. Richards said, "Listen, we've got a faculty meeting in fifteen minutes, and I've got to get ready. So I'll see you there."

The music teacher stood up. "I won't be at the meeting."

Mr. Richards said, "Oh. Then I guess I'll see you tomorrow."

Mr. Meinert nodded and walked out of the office.

Five

TEMPTATIONS

Hart's dad was home in time for dinner, plus he had brought two large pizzas, so everyone was in a pretty good mood.

As Hart bit into a big slice of pepperoni with extra cheese, he debated whether or not to tell his parents about his detentions. And the rubber band incident. This was the weekend Zack's dad had promised to take four of the guys to a hockey game at Madison Square Garden— Rangers against the Bruins. It would be a rotten weekend to get grounded.

So maybe I shouldn't tell.

But he had to serve the two detentions, and his mom was always home from work by three thirty, so that was a problem.

Maybe I could get Kenny Lambert to come over tomorrow after Mom gets home and tell her I had to stay after and do some stuff. Kenny would do that for me. And it wouldn't be a lie. Then I could just take the late bus home at four thirty.

Hart felt like he could get away with not telling. He took a long drink of grape soda, burped, and then quickly said, "Excuse me."

Then he thought, *Except what about the second day? Staying late two days in a row is gonna look fishy. Mom'll want all the details. And what about Sarah being alone for half an hour both days? Mom won't like that.*

Hart knew that if he got caught telling anything less than the whole truth, that would mean *big* trouble. He reached for the sausage-and-mushroom pizza, and he thought, *So maybe I should just tell what happened and take my chances.*

Sarah wiped her mouth with her napkin, put it back in her lap, and said, "So Hart—did you have an interesting day at school?"

Hart almost gagged on a gob of cheese. It was Sarah's tone of voice. She knew. She knew everything, and she was about to rat on him.

Hart's private debate was over.

He swallowed fast and nodded. "Yeah. Actually, school was a little *too* interesting today. Because I did something stupid in chorus. I was messing around with a rubber band,

and it accidentally hit Mr. Meinert. And now I have to stay after school tomorrow. And Friday."

His mom and dad frowned. Sarah smiled.

Hart shrugged and put on a sheepish face. He said, "Yeah, Mr. Meinert got pretty mad, but the principal knew I'd never try to hit anybody on purpose. But I shouldn't have been playing with rubber bands. So that's why I got the detentions. Boy, I'll never do anything like *that* again."

His mom nodded. "Well, I'm glad to hear you say that. I guess I'll have to leave work early tomorrow and Friday."

His dad said, "Two days after school?"

Hart said, "I know. It's a big punishment, but that rubber band hit Mr. Meinert, Dad, and it could have even hit him in the eye. So that's why Mr. Richards made it two days. And he's right. I shouldn't have had those rubber bands at school."

His dad nodded. "Sounds like you've learned a good lesson."

And Hart nodded. "Yeah, I have."

Hart knew he was home free. He took a bite

of pizza, and glanced sideways at his sister.

Sarah was frowning.

On the other side of town Lucy Meinert was talking with her mouth full.

"You know what I think? I think you should quit." She stabbed the air with her chopsticks for emphasis. "Right now. Just quit."

The school day was behind him now, and Mr. Meinert was starting to recover his sense of humor. He smiled as he tipped a white cardboard container and reached in for another helping of stir-fried shrimp.

His wife said, "I'm not kidding, David. I'm making enough money to cover our expenses, and we've got some savings, too. You should walk into that office tomorrow and tell little King Richards that you quit, effective immediately. If the taxpayers in this town want to fire music and art teachers, fine. Let them. Let them go ahead and raise a pack of culturally stunted morons. It'll serve 'em right!"

Mr. Meinert's wife had studied music too, and they had met at college. But Lucy realized she didn't have the patience to be a teacher, and she didn't want to try to earn a living as a singer, either. So she'd gotten a job at a computer software company. The skills that made her good at reading and writing music also made her good at reading and writing computer code. Now she was on her way to becoming a software developer, and she had less patience than ever, especially about the way her husband's school was run.

After a long drink of water she started in again. "Idiots! I mean, if a *company* was running low on money, it wouldn't try to cut costs by firing its most creative people! That's just stupid. What you do is ask *everyone* in the company to take a pay cut, and then everyone pulls together, and they think and they work until they find a way to get more money. And if you really *have* to fire people, then you start near the top. You fire administrators and assistant supervisors and people who don't do the most important work. If you ask me, *that's* what ought to be happening at the schools in Brentbury! And what about the rest of the town government? They could figure out how to find some money if they really believed education was so important. But they're all too stupid and too selfish, so I say you should quit. Tomorrow. Just walk in there and quit."

It was a tempting idea, but Mr. Meinert shook his head and said, "You know I can't do that."

"Why not?" said Lucy. "Afraid you won't get a good recommendation to some other school? What happens at your new school in five or six years when the economy shrinks again? I'll tell you what'll happen—they're going to fire you, just like Brentbury did. Honestly, I don't see why you want to keep teaching. There's no future in it."

He and his wife had had this conversation before, and David Meinert didn't want to argue. It was the only thing his wife didn't quite understand about him.

He had reasons for wanting to be a teacher, personal reasons.

Between the ages of five and sixteen, young Dave Meinert had attended nine different schools in seven different states. As his dad's career advanced, the family had moved to follow the jobs. Dave had spent part of almost every school year as the new kid. During those years the one thing that had always been the same was his music. He had a great voice and perfect pitch, and he was a whiz on the piano. His band and chorus teachers had always made him feel at home. Music had been the one thing Dave could depend on, no matter where they lived.

Two years ago, when David Meinert had gotten the job teaching music in Brentbury, he was thrilled. The town's music program was recognized for excellence all over the state—even around the nation. He and his wife bought a small condo in Brentbury, and David Meinert felt like he had finally come home. He wanted to stay put. He wanted to have a family someday and never make his kids have to move. He wanted to be the teacher who knew how to make the new kids feel welcome. He wanted to teach his neighbors' children and watch them grow up. He wanted to stick around so he could see which kids turned into real musicians, because he knew some of them would. His wife didn't understand why he went to the concerts at the junior high school.

He went because two years ago those children in the eighth grade chorus had been in the sixth grade chorus. They were still *his* kids. And as soon as there was a staff opening, he hoped to move up to the high school chorus program and begin working with more serious singers and more challenging music.

But for now, the sixth grade chorus was his home, and it was a good home. Until a month ago, that is.

Fired. The school district didn't call it that. They called it a RIF, a "reduction in force." He hadn't been fired. He'd been RIFed. It wasn't personal. They weren't getting rid of *him*. They ran out of money, so they got rid of his job. Fired or RIFed, it still amounted to the same thing—they were even the same letters, just rearranged.

And Mr. Richards had been right this afternoon in his office. Mr. Meinert *had* been upset ever since he'd gotten the news. And, yes, his reaction to Hart shooting that rubber band today had been way over the top.

But he couldn't quit. Not that the kids would mind. They'd probably clap and cheer.

This year's chorus was a tough group. Over half of the kids never wanted to work, always resisted every new song. And classroom discipline had never been his best skill anyway.

Still, quitting wasn't an option. It just wouldn't be right.

Lucy was encouraged by her husband's silence. "Really, David, think about it. You put in all those extra hours to find new music. You plan the field trip to the Metropolitan Opera rehearsal every year. You organize the parent volunteers to make programs and decorations for every concert. You tutor kids; you have that new sight-reading group; you spend extra time with the kids who have solos; plus you lend a hand with the sixth grade band, and the orchestra, too. You even write new arrangements—all on your own time. I know you love your work, but you put in at least ten hours of overtime every week. Your salary is pitiful, there's no extra pay for the extra hours, and to show how grateful they are for all this hard work, the school board fires you right in the middle of the school year. It just stinks. And I'm not kidding. You should really think about quitting.

Or at least cutting back. They're just walking all over you. You shouldn't do one bit more than they pay you for."

Mr. Meinert reached across the table and took his wife's hand. "But it's my job. And as long as that's true, then I have to give it my best. I know that sounds stupid to you, but I can't help it. It's just the way I am."

Lucy smiled and shook her head. "I know. And if you were more like me, I probably never would have married you."

It was the best moment of Mr. Meinert's whole day.

Six

SNAP

It was quieter than usual as Mr. Meinert walked into the chorus room on Thursday afternoon. The kids seemed a little tense, a little uncertain.

Mr. Meinert liked it. It was a nice change. As a young man starting his second year of teaching, he was the one who usually felt tense and uncertain. He thought, *Maybe I should explode more often.*

As he took attendance he avoided looking at Hart Evans. Even if he had, their eyes would not have met. Hart was also being careful not to look at Mr. Meinert. He had decided it was a good day to keep a low profile.

The teacher tossed his grade book back onto his desk and said, "Let's start off today with our new Hanukkah song."

A low groan rumbled through the room. Mr. Meinert ignored it. "We're going to have to work on some Hebrew words. Everyone please stand up in front of your desks."

There was more grumbling as the kids stood up. Again, Mr. Meinert ignored it. "We'll start with an easy one—I'm sure you already know it. Take a deep breath, and let me hear everyone say 'Shalom.'"

The word that came back at him sounded a little like "salami."

Mr. Meinert shook his head. "No. No. Listen: Sha-*lom*. Say it."

Again the class made a sound.

Again Mr. Meinert shook his head. "No. Not 'Shiloom.' Sha-*lom*. That's a long *o* sound, like 'home.' Say it clearly with me. One, two, three: Sh—"

Halfway into the first syllable Karen Baker pointed at the windows and yelped, "Look! It's snowing!"

The Hebrew lesson screeched to a stop. Everyone turned to look. "Hey! Snow! Look! It is—it's snowing!"

Tim Miller shouted, "Maybe tomorrow will be a snow day!"

A spontaneous cheer burst out, and the kids rushed toward the long wall of windows.

The music teacher felt the anger rise up in his chest, just as it had yesterday. He wanted to scream and shake his fist at the class. But he resisted.

He walked slowly over to his desk. On his way Mr. Meinert noticed with some satisfaction that one kid had stayed at his seat: Hart Evans.

Mr. Meinert forced himself to sit down behind his desk. He opened a copy of *Music Educator* magazine. He flipped to an article about teaching the music of Bach to high school students. He made himself sit still and stare at the page.

He read the first sentence of the article, and then he read it again, and then a third time. He clenched his teeth and felt his jaw muscles getting tighter and tighter. He said to himself, *I'm not going to yell. I will not lose my temper. The kids know that what they're doing isn't right, and they will stop it. Then we'll begin again. I will sit here and read until everyone sits down and the room is quiet.*

It didn't happen. The kids at the windows stayed there. Ed Kenner opened one and stuck his hand out to try to catch snowflakes. In five seconds all the windows were open.

Around the room small groups of children formed, and kids started talking and laughing. Some of them leaned against the folding desks, and some sat down in clusters on the floor.

Even though he didn't look up from his magazine, Mr. Meinert could tell kids were sneaking quick looks at him. As three minutes crawled by, Mr. Meinert realized that since he didn't look mad, didn't look like a threat, the kids were perfectly happy to pretend he wasn't there. He had ceased to exist. Everyone was perfectly happy to do nothing. Apparently, doing nothing was a lot more fun than singing in the sixth grade chorus.

Mr. Meinert did not normally do things on the spur of the moment. He liked to plan. He liked to make lists. He liked to organize his thoughts. He liked to think, and then think again.

Not this time.

It was partly because of what had happened the day before—the rubber band incident. It was partly because of everything his wife had said to him at dinner yesterday. It was partly because he hadn't slept well last night and had been feeling lousy all day. And it was partly because Mr. Meinert was sick and tired of trying to make this mob of kids sing when most of them clearly did not want to.

For a dozen different reasons, in Mr. Meinert's mind something snapped. He jumped to his feet, grabbed a piece of chalk, and began writing on the board.

Kids turned to watch.

In tall letters he wrote *HOL*—but he pressed so hard and wrote so fast that the chalk broke. Mr. Meinert threw the yellow stub to the floor, snatched another piece, and kept pushing until he had written these words on the chalkboard:

HOLIDAY CONCERT
December 22, 7 PM

Quiet spread across the room like an oil spill. Kids began tiptoeing back to their seats. His shoulders tense and his jaw still clenched, Mr. Meinert kept writing.

Sixth Grade Orchestra—20 minutes
Sixth Grade Band—20 minutes
Sixth Grade Chorus—30 minutes

Mr. Meinert underlined the bottom words three times, and each time the chalk made a sound that would have made a dog run out of the room.

Then he turned to look at the class. Each child was seated, every eye was on his face.

Mr. Meinert spoke slowly, pronouncing each word carefully. "Thirty minutes. That's how long the chorus will perform during the holiday concert. All your parents will be there. Grandparents will be there. Probably brothers and sisters. It's the biggest concert of the year. Well, guess what?" He slowly raised his right arm and with his fingers stretched out, palm down, he swept his hand from side to side, pointing at the whole chorus. "This holiday concert, this thirty-minute performance? It's all *yours*."

Someone let out a nervous laugh.

Mr. Meinert spun toward the sound. "Think *this* is funny? Well, just wait until December twenty-second, a little after seven thirty. That's when the *real* fun begins. You see, no one's coming to that concert to see me. I'm just the music teacher. Everyone is coming to see *you*, to listen to you. To watch the wonderful program. So *that's* when things will start to get fun. Because from this moment on, the holiday concert is all up to you. To *you*. Not me. It's not my concert. It's *your* concert. You don't like the songs I've picked? Fine. Pick your own. You don't like the way I run the rehearsals? No problem. Run them yourselves. You don't want to sing at all? Then you can just stand up in front of your parents and the rest of the school for half an hour and do nothing. Who knows what will happen on December twenty-second? Not me. Right now, there is only one thing that I'm sure of. On December twenty-second a little after seven thirty in the evening, I will make sure that all of you are on that stage in the auditorium. What happens once you're there . . . that's all up to *you*."

Mr. Meinert turned around, looked at the wall calendar, then picked up a piece of chalk and wrote on the board:

23 DAYS

"Next Thursday is Thanksgiving. Counting today, there are twenty-three class periods left before the day of *your* concert. There won't be any after-school rehearsals like we had for the Halloween concert, no dress rehearsal the night before. You have only these twenty-three class periods. You've learned four songs so far. But of course, you might want to toss them out and choose different songs. All that is now up to you. So. Have a nice concert."

Mr. Meinert turned and took three quick steps to his desk. He leaned over and pushed. The metal legs screeched on the floor as he slid the desk to the far right side of the room and then spun it around to face the wall. He walked back, rolled his chair over to the desk and sat down, his back to the class. He picked up his *Music Educator* magazine and began to read the article about teaching Bach.

For the first time in more than a month, Mr. Meinert felt great.

Seven

THE VOICE OF THE PEOPLE

Hart sat still, hands folded in front of him. But his eyes darted around the music room, looking for clues, watching for danger, trying to see what was coming next.

The room was silent. Mr. Meinert had been reading at his desk for almost four minutes. Hart studied the back of the man's head, looking for anger in his neck and shoulders, examining the way he held his magazine. If another storm was coming, Hart wanted to see it in time to duck for cover.

Hart didn't trust the quiet. Mr. Meinert was a funnel cloud. Any second now he might whip around and start ripping things apart. Hart wasn't about to put himself in the path of another tornado. Yesterday's direct hit had been plenty.

Off to his right Hart heard a trickle of whispers.

"What are we supposed to do?"

"I don't know. I guess just sit here."

"Is he serious?"

"I . . . I think so."

"He said we can do anything we want. So can we?"

"I don't know. Now be quiet!"

It got quiet again, but silent children are like a rising river. Sooner or later the water spills over the banks.

More whispers. They grew louder, and then came the low talking.

Still Mr. Meinert sat and read his magazine. He wanted to leap from his chair. The urge to take charge of his classroom was almost overpowering. But he forced himself to sit and read.

As the low talking spread, a few kids kept saying, "Shhh . . . SHHHH," but the shushing couldn't hold back the flow.

Then, on the other side of the room, someone must have said something funny. Two kids started laughing, and the flood broke loose.

The noise level in the room rose so fast it took Mr. Meinert's breath away. And as more kids talked and laughed, others had to talk still louder and louder in order to be heard above the rising clamor. For a moment Mr. Meinert was sure that the whole sixth grade was packed into the room. He wanted to spin his chair around and give the kids his most withering stare, but he made himself sit still, made himself keep reading.

After three minutes the noise was deafening. The room wasn't out of control, but it was close. Three or four guys had started playing baseball, with some wadded up paper for a ball and a music book for a bat. A cell phone tweedled, and a girl on one side of the room pulled it out of her purse, jammed it to her ear, and then spun around and waved at her friend who had called from thirty feet away. A few groups of kids had gone back to the windows to watch the snow come down. Four girls sat on the floor and began playing Rock, Paper, Scissors—dangerously close to the three guys kicking a Hacky Sack. Everyone else was just milling around, talking and laughing.

Hart hadn't budged from his chair. His desk was like his lifeboat, a safe place to watch from. Only four other kids besides Hart were still sitting at their desks. Two of them had begun doing homework, and the other two kids—Colleen and Ross—were arguing. Colleen Hester was almost yelling at Ross Eastman, and he was shaking his head and making a face back at her. Hart didn't care much for either of them, especially Colleen. Too bossy. As Hart watched, Colleen and Ross stood up and walked down front to Mr. Meinert's desk.

It was too loud to hear anything, but Hart saw Colleen say something to Mr. Meinert. He looked up at Colleen, and also at Ross, and then Mr. Meinert smiled and nodded and shrugged his shoulders all at the same time. He turned back to his magazine.

Colleen tugged on Ross's shirt and pulled him with her until they stood next to the electric piano at the front of the room.

"Hey everybody!" Colleen yelled. "Hey, listen. Please, everybody—listen—QUIET!"

The room calmed down a little, and Colleen said, "Ross and I want to say something, okay? We just talked to Mr. Meinert, and he said if we wanted, we could be in charge of the concert. So we want to get started now, okay?"

Janie Kingston didn't care much for Colleen either. She stood up and said, "I don't think that's fair. How come you should be in charge? Just because you talked to Mr. Meinert first?"

And then Tim Miller climbed up on the seat of his desk and made a goofy face and said, "Hey, maybe *I* should be in charge— what d'ya think, guys?" And four of Tim's friends started chanting, "WE WANT TIM! WE WANT TIM!"

Ross raised his hands and shouted, "Guys, shut up! C'mon, shut up!"

Tim yelled back, "No, *you* shut up!" and for fifteen seconds about forty kids yelled "Shut up!" at one another.

The shouting burned out, and when it got a little quieter, Ross said, "Janie's right, okay? Everything has to be fair. So first everyone's got to sit down. Then we'll have an election to see who runs the concert. You can vote for anyone—like for me, or Janie, or for Colleen."

"Hey!" yelled Tim. "What about me?" And his friends started chanting again, "TIM! TIM! TIM!"

Ross grinned. "Sure. Tim too. But everyone

has to sit down. And the person with the most votes wins."

Ross grabbed four or five pieces of paper from his notebook, ripped them into little squares, and started passing them out.

As quickly as the room had gotten noisy, it got quiet again. Everyone took a ballot and began writing.

Hart almost voted for Janie, but at the last minute he wrote Ross's name. Ross was sort of a brainhead, but he was still a pretty good guy.

Colleen took a small drum from a shelf at the front of the room, turned it upside down, and dropped her ballot in. Then she walked up and down the rows until everyone had put one ballot into the drum.

She took the drum to a table at the front of the room and dumped it out. When she started to unfold the ballots, someone yelled, "Hey—no fair! Someone else should count!"

And another kid yelled, "Yeah, Mr. Meinert should count." Around the room, kids nodded and said, "Yeah! Mr. Meinert!" "Yeah, 'cause he won't cheat!" "It should be Mr. Meinert!"

Mr. Meinert, still reading his magazine, shook his head.

Colleen walked over to him and said, "*Please*, Mr. Meinert? Everybody wants you to."

Mr. Meinert was actually relieved, glad to be taking charge of his classroom again. But he didn't show it. He put down his magazine, slowly stood up, and rolled his desk chair over to the table. He sat down in front of the heap of ballots and began unfolding each one, sorting the different names into separate piles. The only sound in the room was crinkling paper.

When the last ballot was unfolded and sorted, Mr. Meinert began counting. He counted the ballots in the first pile, and then counted them a second time. Then he pulled a pad of Post-it notes out of his pocket, wrote down a number, peeled off the note, and stuck it onto the pile. Then he started counting the second pile. There were almost seventy-five ballots, so it took him about ten minutes to count them all.

When he was done, Mr. Meinert looked at the numbers he'd written on each pile of ballots.

Then he picked up what looked like the biggest stack and counted them again. And then he counted the other big stack.

Mr. Meinert stood up. He took a deep breath and let it out slowly. He looked around the room, enjoying the silence, enjoying how completely he had everyone's attention.

Speaking slowly, he said, "First, I want to thank those few students who voted for me. It was a kind thought, but your votes were wasted. I've already told you that between now and Christmas vacation I will be in this room only as an observer. Therefore, it is now my duty to announce the results of this free and fair election. The new chorus director for this year's holiday concert is none other than our very own . . . Hart Evans."

Eight

DIRECTOR

After Mr. Meinert's announcement the room was quiet, but only for a second.

"No way!" Hart gripped the sides of his desk. He shook his head and looked around the room. "No way! I'm not gonna be the chorus director—I wasn't even *in* this election—no way!"

Colleen jumped to her feet and said, "I can be the director, okay? I know I can do it. And I'll do a good job at it too."

Mr. Meinert said, "Colleen, please sit down." Then, turning to Hart, he said, "You already *are* the new director, Hart. We all heard the rules. Ross said that the whole chorus could vote for anyone. That's what he said. And you didn't complain about that. And like everyone else, you went along with the rules. And you voted too, right?"

Hart gulped. "Well, yeah . . . sure, I voted. But I didn't want to get elected." Hart pointed toward Colleen and Ross. "One of them ought to do it. They're the ones who want to."

Mr. Meinert shrugged. "Too late. They weren't elected. *You* were, and that's that." He pulled his chair away from the table where the ballots were and began pushing it back toward his desk. "So have a very nice concert." Mr. Meinert sat down, opened his magazine, and began to read again.

Hart didn't know what to do. All the kids were looking at him. He felt embarrassed.

Colleen hurried over and stood in front of him. "What do you want us to do first? You heard Mr. Meinert. We only have twenty-three days. We have to get started."

Hart looked up at her. Colleen put her hands on her hips and said, "Well? What should we do?"

Hart said, "You know that song 'I'm a Little Teapot'? How about you walk down to the front of the room and sing that song for everybody. That would be a good start."

Hart's wisecrack got a pretty big laugh, and around the room kids started whispering and talking.

Colleen made a pinched face at him. "You think you're *so* funny. Really—what *are* you going to do? We have to get started."

Hart ignored Colleen and stood up. Waiting for the room to get quiet, Hart thought, *If Mr. Meinert wants to be all tough and make me do this, then I can play games too.*

Hart said, "Okay, listen everybody. As the new chorus director, I declare that this is a free period. And tomorrow will be a free period too. Chorus is now a free period." And then Hart sat down.

A spontaneous cheer filled the room. "Yaaay!" "Woo-woo!" "*Awe*some! This is great!" "Yeah—cool!"

Still standing there in front of Hart with her hands on her hips, Colleen said, "You are *so* immature!" She turned and stomped back to her desk.

In less than a minute the room was as loud as it had been before the election.

Reading at his desk with his ears wide open, once again it took all Mr. Meinert's will power to keep himself from leaping to his feet. He wanted to sweep his eyes across the crowd. He wanted to shout, *Silence!* and snap the room to order. But he thought, *No, I'm not going to explode. I'm not going to rant and rave and look like an angry fool again. I'll wait. I'll wait until the noise and the disorder and the confusion overpowers them. A free period—hah! Nobody can stand chaos for long, not even sixth graders. It might take a day or two, but they'll all get sick of it. Hart and his fan club, they think chorus is a big joke? Well, the joke's on them!*

By the time these thoughts had run through his mind, Mr. Meinert was trying to keep from smiling, and what he really wanted to do was laugh out loud. Hart Evans, the Rubber Bandit— Hart was now in charge of the chorus, in charge of the big concert! It was too perfect.

Mr. Meinert knew he was being petty and childish. He knew he was being unprofessional. But at that moment he didn't care. Mr. Meinert was planning to enjoy himself. Soon would come the part where Hart and everyone else would be pleading, begging him to take charge of the chorus and organize the concert. And after they had groveled and whined long enough, he would slowly let himself be talked into it. It was going to be so much *fun*.

There was only one small problem with this analysis: Mr. Meinert did not know Hart Evans as well as he thought he did.

In fact, none of them knew Hart Evans as well as they thought they did—including Hart Evans himself.

Nine

DETENTION

"Palmer Intermediate, Mrs. Hood speaking. Will you please hold a moment?"

It was a little before three o'clock. The hallways had gotten quiet, but the office was still jumping. Moms and dads had come to drop off notes or pick up kids, and a steady stream of teachers rushed in and out. The nurse went bustling through with a girl who had skinned her knee, and the school secretary was trying to help everyone while she juggled three phone calls.

Hart trudged up to the counter and waited.

Putting one hand over the telephone mouthpiece, the secretary raised her eyebrows. "Yes?"

Hart whispered, "Um . . . I'm here for detention."

Mrs. Hood shook her head. "Talk louder, dear."

"Detention," said Hart, his face turning

pink. "I have to serve a detention."

She pushed a clipboard and a pen toward him. After Hart had written his name and the time, Mrs. Hood pointed toward the bench with one long red fingernail.

Hart sat down and dug a novel out of his backpack, flipped it open to his bookmark, leaned against the wall, and began to read. The noisy office and the school with all its clocks disappeared.

The moment Carson knew something was wrong, it was already too late. First came a muffled explosion, then the screech of tires. The small car bucked and shuddered as he fought to get it back under control. The left fender scraped the tunnel wall and sparks splashed the windshield, almost blinding him. Too fast, too fast! But the brake pedal had turned to mush! Carson struggled against the steering wheel, struggled to keep the car from veering into an oncoming truck. It was no use. As if a giant hand had taken hold. . . .

"Well. It's Mr. Evans."

Hart looked up from his book and blinked. Mr. Meinert stood there in front of him, smiling. "You seem very relaxed. I thought I'd find you madly preparing for your big concert. With so much responsibility hanging over *my* head, I usually get pretty anxious, all tied up in knots. But this year I think I'm really going to enjoy the holidays."

Mr. Meinert turned away and walked over to the wall of teacher mailboxes. He pulled a stack of papers out of his cubbyhole, and as he riffled through them he began humming "Frosty the Snowman."

Hart tried to get back into his book, but Mr. Meinert's humming was distracting. Annoying, too. And the guy was taking his time at the mailboxes, carefully looking over every piece of mail, every memo, every note.

Finally the music teacher turned to go, and as he started out the door he smiled at Hart and said, "I'm looking forward to chorus tomorrow."

It was the combination of the smile and Mr. Meinert's tone of voice. It reminded Hart of his sister Sarah, and that little comment made him feel like he'd just been poked in the ribs.

Hart suddenly felt brave—which can be dangerous for a kid serving detention in the office. He smiled back at Mr. Meinert and said, "Chorus? Oh, you mean *free period*. I'm looking forward to free period, too."

Mr. Meinert stopped. He came over and stood in front of Hart. "That free period business? That's not a good idea, Hart."

Still feeling much too brave, Hart said, "Well . . . me being the chorus director? That's not a good idea either. Someone else should do it." Hart paused a second and then said, "*You* should do it. You're the real director."

Mr. Meinert suddenly liked the way this conversation was going. He said, "How about this: If you can convince the class tomorrow that I should be in charge again, then we'll get back to work. Just tell everybody that the job is too big for a kid to handle. That should do it. Of course, they might still want chorus to be a free period. But that's your problem. Fair enough?"

Hart nodded. "Sure." It sounded like an

easy way out. He said, "That's what I'll do."

"All right then," said Mr. Meinert. "See you tomorrow." And he left the office.

As Mr. Meinert walked away Hart could hear him whistling a melody—*"Deck the halls with boughs of holly, fa la la la la, la la la la."*

Hart felt relieved, but not quite as jolly as Mr. Meinert did. Hart still had plenty of detention left.

He tucked his book away, rested his elbows on his knees, and put his chin in his hands. He sat there looking down at the green and brown speckles of the office carpet, thinking and thinking. And the more he thought, the more he liked the idea of Mr. Meinert taking charge of the concert again. Any other solution would just lead to trouble—probably more detentions, too.

But the feeling that he'd been poked in the ribs wouldn't go away. It almost felt like Mr. Meinert had tricked him. But how? Hart couldn't figure it out.

The idea that everything would just go back to normal in chorus—that part of the deal seemed fine. Better than fine . . . wonderful.

Hart knew he did *not* want to be in charge of this concert. Or any concert, ever. No way. He wanted to hide in the back row of the chorus and mumble through the songs like he always did.

And all he had to do was stand up in class tomorrow and tell everyone that organizing the concert was impossible. And then ask Mr. Meinert to take charge again. Not so bad. He knew he could do that, and he knew he could get the class to go along, too. But something still didn't feel quite right to Hart. His thoughts went round and round.

Thinking back to the class period, Hart remembered what had happened after he said Colleen or Ross should be the director. Mr. Meinert had said, "They weren't elected. *You* were."

Hart thought about that, about being elected. He had been elected, and without asking anybody for a single vote. *How come the kids elected me? Because I'm popular, that's how come.*

Hart had always known he was pretty popular. But this election? That proved it. And that made him feel good.

Then Hart thought, *But it was also sort of a joke. Everyone thought it would be funny if I was the chorus director. Especially after that rubber band business. They thought it would be funny.*

Hart smiled and nodded. It *was* funny.

Then Hart sat up straight on the bench in the office, sat up so fast that he almost banged his head against the wall. *Mr. Meinert . . .* he *thinks it's funny, too! Me, being the director! And me standing up tomorrow and saying I can't do it—he thinks that'll be the funniest part of all! I'm squirming, and he's having a blast! He's going to be laughing the whole time!*

Hart sat on the bench staring straight ahead, nodding slowly, his eyes bright. The look on his face was so intense that when Mrs. Hood glanced at him, she stood up and said, "Hart, are you all right?"

Surprised, Hart looked at her blankly for a second. "Me?" he asked.

Mrs. Hood said, "Yes. Are you okay?"

Hart nodded, and with a crooked little smile he said, "I'm just *fine.*"

Ten

BRILLIANCE

On Friday Mr. Meinert called the chorus to order as usual. He took attendance as usual. Then he said, "Hart, it's all yours."

Right away Tim Miller chirped, "Yippee—free period!"

Before a lot more cheering could break out, Hart stood up and said, "Hold it, everybody. Listen a minute . . . listen."

It got completely quiet. The sudden silence surprised Hart almost as much as it surprised Mr. Meinert.

Hart froze for a second or two and his face started to get red. But he gulped and said, "I . . . I know that me . . . you know, me getting elected and everything? I know it was sort of a joke—and it's pretty funny."

Tim Miller wagged his head and went, "Har, har, har! Haw, haw, haw!" exaggerating a big laugh. The rest of the kids laughed too, but when Hart raised his hand, everyone got quiet.

Again Hart was amazed by how quickly the kids quieted down for him. And again so was Mr. Meinert.

Hart said, "It's funny and all, but the concert's really got to happen. Like, we've really got to stand up in the auditorium in front of everybody for a long time and . . . and do something."

"Hey!" said Tim. "I can dance! Look!" And he jumped out of his chair and started swinging his hips and waving his arms around.

Hart grinned and nodded, and then he said, "Yeah, but can you do that all by yourself up on the stage for half an hour . . . and with your grandma watching?" That got a big laugh, and Tim took a bow and sat down.

Hart said, "So I started thinking last night. And I don't think we better have any free periods. Because making a concert happen, it won't be easy."

Tim and a few of his pals said, "Hey, no fair!" "Yeah, no fair!" But most of the kids were listening to Hart and nodding, right there with him.

Mr. Meinert was listening too. This was the part he'd been waiting for.

Hart said, "So I've got a question for Mr. Meinert—a very important question."

Mr. Meinert stood up and faced Hart. The music teacher was careful to keep his face under control, to keep his expression neutral. He didn't want to appear too happy about being asked to be the director again. And he wanted to be able to look surprised when Hart asked him.

Hart cleared his throat. The room went still as a comic strip. Hart said, "I want to know, Mr. Meinert—because, you know how you said we could do anything for our part of the big concert?" Mr. Meinert nodded, and Hart went on, "So what I want to know is—if the chorus's part of the concert went on for *more* than thirty minutes, will we get in trouble? 'Cause I've got tons of great ideas about cool stuff we could do, but I don't know how it can all fit into just half an hour."

Before Mr. Meinert could open his mouth, Ed Kenner called out "What kind of stuff, Hart?"

"Yeah," said Colleen, "do you mean like costumes? And decorations, like snowflakes, or stars? 'Cause I've been thinking about the concert too."

Hart nodded, grabbing a clipboard from his backpack. "Yeah, lots of costumes, and stuff like drum solos and maybe karaoke with the audience. And maybe somebody could dress up like Elvis in a Santa suit."

"Me!" yelled Tim. "Me! I can be a perfect Elvis!" And he got up and started dancing again.

Jenna waved both hands. "Hart! Hart! At home we've got these two dreidel costumes my aunt made—like you spin around in them and you get all dizzy and fall down, but it's okay because they're made of this soft rubber stuff. They're really funny—could we use them do you think?"

"Sure, sounds great!" said Hart. "There's a *ton* of stuff we could do!"

The room began buzzing, and six or seven other kids were trying to get Hart's attention. But he held up his hand and turned back to Mr. Meinert. Again it got quiet, and Hart said, "So what do you think, Mr. Meinert? Can our part of the concert go a little longer?"

Mr. Meinert was having trouble with his face. It would not behave. His mouth was smiling—almost smiling. But not his eyes. No smile there at all. His voice wasn't much better. He growled, "Well . . . it's not good to go on too long."

"But everybody's coming to see *us*, right?" asked Hart. "Like you said?"

Mr. Meinert nodded slightly.

"So," said Hart, "it ought to be okay as long as we don't go *way* too long, right?"

Mr. Meinert's face was in big trouble now. No smile at all. "Yes . . . I guess so."

"Great!" said Hart. He turned back to the class. "Now, we've really got to get serious, okay? So Colleen, could you be sort of like the stage director? I know you could do a really great job." Colleen smiled and nodded, and Hart said, "And could you maybe get some kids together and come up with ideas about decorations? And costumes, too? Because we can do whatever we want. It doesn't have to look like a regular old concert. And then we can all talk about the ideas on Monday. And does anybody have one of those karaoke computer programs?"

Ann and Lee raised their hands. Hart nodded and said, "Great . . . over the weekend you should both look at them and see if there are any Christmas type songs. 'Cause that could really be fun. And listen, everybody, listen. We should probably sing some regular concert songs too, because, you know, like, we're the chorus. So everyone should make a list of some songs that might be good, and then we can write them all on the board on Monday and decide which ones to sing. And if anyone wants to sing a solo, that'd be great . . . but no one *has* to. Now, how many kids here know how to play an instrument?"

Completely ignored, Mr. Meinert walked over and sat down at his desk. He tried to act like he wasn't interested. But he was. He also tried to act like his feelings weren't hurt. But they were. And he was still having plenty of trouble with his face.

But more than that, his mind was spinning. He could not believe what he'd just seen. Four minutes! It had taken Hart Evans only four minutes to get the whole group excited about working together. And not only that—everyone had practically cheered about doing *more* than they had to.

Watching out of the corner of his eye, Mr. Meinert saw Hart hurry over to Ross, heard Hart use a good loud voice as he said, "Hey, do you think you could be in charge of organizing all the music on Monday? Can I count on you?" Ross smiled and nodded, excited, honored that Hart would give him such an important job.

Brilliant! The word jumped into Mr. Meinert's mind. *The kid's already got Colleen and Ross working for him. Brilliant! And he's even got Tim Miller focused—still wacky, but focused. Amazing!*

As if to prove the point, Tim ran over to Mr. Meinert's desk, panting and bobbing from side to side. "Mr. Meinert? Mr. Meinert? You know that thing Elvis does when he sings, you know, like with his upper lip? Is it sort of like . . . like this?" And Tim pushed his face into a sneer.

Mr. Meinert smiled and nodded. "Almost. Rent an Elvis movie this weekend, maybe *Blue Hawaii*. You'll get it."

"Cool!" said Tim, and he spun off into orbit again, playing an air guitar.

Over the next thirty-five minutes the music room did not plunge into chaos. Instead, small groups formed up, some sitting on the floor, some around the tables down front, and some at desks pulled into the corners. There was a lot of loud talking, a lot of moving around, and some arguing and shouting—laughing, too. There was plenty of noise, but most of it had a purpose.

And whenever Mr. Meinert glanced up, there was Hart in the thick of it all, walking from cluster to cluster with his clipboard, making notes, making jokes, making friends, pulling the whole chorus together. And smiling.

Because Hart Evans was not having any trouble with *his* face. No trouble at all.

Eleven

FEELINGS

At three fifteen on Friday Mr. Meinert sat alone in the music room. He slumped in his chair, staring at the wall. A couple of nights ago his wife had told him what he ought to do. And now he agreed with her. He wanted to quit—just quit.

Oh, yeah, he thought, *I'm a great teacher! What was I thinking? All that grandstanding. "The whole concert is up to you now, kids." And when Hart steps up to the challenge and it starts looking like they might actually pull something together, what do I do? I get all mad—and then I sit around with my feelings hurt like a big baby. I am such a loser! I . . . I give up!*

At this same moment Hart sat alone on the long bench in the office. He was dealing with some feelings of his own. Part of him wanted to grin and cheer about what he'd pulled off in chorus today. The scene had played out perfectly. Mr. Meinert had been expecting one thing, and he had done the opposite. He had sprung a perfect trap. And Mr. Meinert knew that he'd done it on purpose. That look on Mr. Meinert's face when he'd popped the surprises about the concert? Priceless! The guy had tried to hide it. Didn't work. The anger was right there for anybody to see.

But along with the anger, Hart had seen something else—just a glimpse before it was hidden. Hart had seen some sadness in Mr. Meinert's eyes. Some hurt. And part of Hart didn't feel so good about that.

Still, Hart said to himself, *Mr. Meinert had it coming. All I did was what he was trying to do to me. I just did it better, that's all. And if he's mad about it . . . well, too bad.*

Hart tried to let that be the end of it, tried to do some math homework. But he couldn't stop thinking about it.

Ten minutes later Mr. Meinert had his coat on. He grabbed his briefcase, picked up a small stack of mail from his desk, locked the music room door, and headed for the office.

Mr. Meinert had one hand on the office door before he saw Hart, sitting there on the bench below the clock. Mr. Meinert stopped, turned quickly, and hurried down the hall toward the parking lot. He shoved the envelopes into his coat pocket. The mail could wait. He'd had enough of Hart Evans for one day.

He was almost at the double doors when he heard, "Hey! Mr. Meinert!"

It was Hart.

Mr. Meinert turned around. Acting surprised, he said, "Oh, it's you. I'm sort of in a hurry. Can this wait till Monday?"

Hart trotted down the hall until he stood right in front of the music teacher. He did his best to smile, a little out of breath. He panted harder than he needed to and fanned his face, stalling for time. Hart wasn't sure what he was going to say to Mr. Meinert. But he felt like he ought to say something—anything. So he just started talking.

"Um . . . I just wanted to say . . . well, what I did in chorus today? I know it wasn't what we talked about yesterday. And I think it kind of made you mad. And I'm sorry about that. 'Cause I guess I knew it would . . . make you mad, I mean." Hart gulped, and made himself keep talking, his mind barely half a step ahead of his words. "But . . . but if I made you mad today . . . that means you weren't just sort of *willing* to do the concert, right? I mean, you got mad because . . . because you still really *want* to run the concert, right?"

Mr. Meinert did not want to be having this conversation. He didn't want to answer Hart's question. He was tempted to turn his back and go out the door.

But he didn't walk away from the question. Instead Mr. Meinert did what he'd learned to do all his life: He told the truth.

He nodded slightly. "Yes, that's true, Hart. I would have been happy to take charge of the chorus again."

Hart said, "Really?" Then, thinking fast, he said, "That's . . . that's *great*! I am *so* glad to hear you say that! Because I *think* we could put on some kind of a concert—just the kids, I mean— but I don't really know much about music. None of us does, not like you. So . . . so if we get in trouble, like with the music, will you help us? I mean, can I count on you?"

Mr. Meinert remembered what he'd seen during chorus earlier today, remembered Hart's talk with Ross. And he thought, *Hart Evans is recruiting me! He's inviting me to be on his team, just like he did with Ross!* The music teacher stood there with his mouth open, amazed at the nerve of this kid.

Still, it felt like an honest invitation, so he gave Hart an honest answer. "Yes," Mr. Meinert said. "Yes, you can. You can count on me."

Hart smiled and stuck out his hand, and after a half second's hesitation, Mr. Meinert shook it, surprised by the strength he felt there, the energy and the sincerity.

"Great!" said Hart. "Well . . . I've got to go back to detention. So . . . see you Monday."

Mr. Meinert nodded, turned, and walked out the door, heading toward his car.

As he pulled in a deep breath of cold November air, he had to smile. And just as it had earlier, one word jumped into his mind: *Brilliant!*

Twelve

AS VIEWED FROM ABOVE

The chorus room was not the only part of Palmer Intermediate School that was buzzing with fresh activity. Hart had been elected sixth grade chorus director at approximately 1:30 on Thursday, November 18. At 3:30 that same afternoon Mr. Richards had gotten a phone call.

"Mr. Richards?"

"Yes?"

"This is Melanie Baker. I'm Karen Baker's mom, and she's in the chorus this year. Well, today after school Karen told me that a boy named . . . is it Hart? Or maybe it's Bart . . . well, anyway, some sixth grade boy is the director of the chorus now. And she said that the music teacher just lets the kids go wild. Have you heard anything about this?"

He had not heard, but Mr. Richards didn't say that. He said, "Mr. Meinert is the chorus director, and he's an exceptional teacher. I know the chorus is working hard to prepare for the holiday concert these days, and if Mr. Meinert has asked the students to take part in planning the concert, then the room might be a little more active than usual. Is your daughter upset about this?"

Mrs. Baker laughed. "Who, Karen? She'd die if she knew I was calling you. She loves how crazy it is, and she told me that tomorrow she's taking her CD player and some little speakers so she and her friend can practice dancing. It's me, *I'm* the one who's worried. It just sounds a little out of control."

The principal assured Mrs. Baker that no part of the intermediate school was out of control at any time, and that he would keep a close eye on the progress of the chorus.

The second phone call was waiting on hold before Mrs. Baker had said good-bye.

"Hi, Mr. Richards, it's Maureen Kendall. If we can, I'd like to request a schedule change for my son, Thomas. He'd like to switch to a study hall after lunch, maybe in the library? Right now he has chorus during that period, but from what he's told me about that class, I think he'd do better if he could have a quiet study time instead."

The principal explained that midyear schedule changes were not possible, and then he assured Mrs. Kendall that chorus was the right place for Thomas, and that any confusion in that room was only a temporary condition.

By the time he left for the day, the principal had spoken with two other parents about the situation in the sixth grade chorus.

Mr. Richards was not a naturally nosy person. But he was responsible for the quality of learning and the daily safety of every student, and if there was a problem in the chorus room, or in any room, he needed to know about it. So he decided that the next day he would do a little snooping.

Friday after lunch, instead of heading straight back to the office from the cafeteria, Mr. Richards walked outside across the playground, back inside through the gym door, down the hallway past the media center, into the auditorium, across the stage, and out the door on the other side. He was headed toward the chorus room.

He heard the class the second he turned the corner into the long hallway, and the noise increased with each step he took. And when the principal peeked through the window of the closed door, it didn't look good. Kids were sitting around on the floor, chairs and tables were pulled into disorganized groups all over the place, the noise was far above any acceptable level, and one boy was running around the room acting like he was playing a guitar. And in the midst of this mess, there was Mr. Meinert, sitting calmly at his desk, reading. This was not right, not at all.

Mr. Richards put a hand on the doorknob, but then his eye happened to stop on Hart Evans. The boy was half hidden, squatting next to some girls who were sitting on the floor. Hart nodded as one girl talked, and he looked from face to face as the others commented, and he took careful notes on a clipboard.

Then Hart stood up, walked to a group of three boys who were arguing, listened for a minute, and then said something. The boys listened, nodded, Hart made a few notes, and then he moved on.

Mr. Richards knew what he was watching. He'd been involved with work like this most of his professional life. This was committee work. And Hart Evans was clearly the chairperson. Yes, it was noisy, and somebody should be sitting on that boy who was dancing around the room. But the situation wasn't dangerous, and it was not out of control. He'd have to keep an eye on things, but that was all in a day's work.

As Mr. Richards walked slowly back to his office, he congratulated himself on being so broad-minded and flexible. *Who's afraid of a little messiness? Not me. Education is all about experimentation. That's what makes this job exciting.*

But in the back of the principal's mind, another thought was whispering as well. *That Meinert—he is creative, but he can be pretty emotional. I sure hope he knows what he's doing.*

Thirteen

SMOOTH SAILING

After his surprise election—and after he had recruited Mr. Meinert to his team—Hart's first seven class periods as director had been exhilarating. It wasn't the sixth grade chorus anymore. It was The Chorus According to Hart. No endless rehearsing. No unreasonable demands. And during those first seven classes, no singing. Chorus had become cool, and the holiday concert was going to prove it. The concert was going to be amazing, fantastic, wonderful—even fun.

Hart urged everybody to think big, think free, think bold. He urged everyone to break out of the mold. *This* holiday concert was going to be one of a kind, once in a lifetime, one for the ages. Hart told the kids they could do it, and they believed him. He was the fearless captain, steering their ship into uncharted waters. The skies were blue, the winds were fair, and the gentle waves rolled on toward the cheerful horizon. It was smooth sailing. Under Hart's command, ideas welled up like a rising tide, and each one was welcomed aboard.

Hart smiled and nodded as Jim Barker explained his exciting plan to rearrange the whole auditorium. Jim had diagrams he'd made on his computer. There would be three runways out to a stage in the very center of the room, and the chorus would be surrounded by the audience, and there would be lights shining in from everywhere, just like on that talent show on TV. Jim had found only one problem so far: Every seat in the auditorium was bolted to the concrete floor. Hart told Jim to keep thinking.

Hart smiled and nodded as Lisa Morton explained how she wanted to fly around the stage on wires like Peter Pan, except dressed up like an angel, or maybe one of Santa's elves, or maybe a snowflake with arms and legs. Hart helped Lisa do some quick Internet research, which showed that the arrangements for that kind of flying would cost about twelve thousand dollars—not including the cost of special insurance in case of injury or death. Lisa said she'd talk to her dad about the money.

Hart smiled and nodded as Olivia Lambert and Shannon Roda described their dance routine. They were two of the prettiest girls in sixth grade, and they were in ballet class together, and they wanted to do the dance of the Marzipan Shepherdesses from *The Nutcracker*. They already had their costumes, and if the sixth grade orchestra couldn't learn the music in time, they had a CD and a really big boom box. And Shannon's mom had volunteered to start and stop the music at the right places. It sounded like a lot of messing around, but Hart liked the way Shannon kept smiling at him, so he smiled back and kept on nodding.

Every day kids came to him with new ideas, all of them interesting, all of them creative. Kids were even calling him at home to ask for his opinion. Jasmine Royce had prepared a gymnastic routine to the music of "Winter Wonderland." Three guys wanted to come out in costumes and perform "The Chipmunk Song." Five girls wanted to dress up like a boy band and do a hip-hop version of "Rudolph the Red-Nosed Reindeer." And Captain Hart

Evans smiled and nodded and took careful notes in the ship's log, and he promised to give every idea his careful consideration.

Hart was glad to have Colleen on board as second in command. She was a practical, no-nonsense person, and she and her staging committee had gotten right to work. They'd come up with good ideas for decorations, simple and doable. There were going to be stars and streamers everywhere—gold and silver, blue and white, red and green, hundreds and hundreds of them—hanging on the curtains, suspended from the ceiling, filling every doorway, covering the walls. The committee had sketches and plans, lists of materials, and a schedule for making everything—it all looked fantastic.

Allison Kim was on Colleen's committee, and she had been watching a show on TV about a French circus, *Cirque du Soleil*. She loved their costumes, so that got her thinking. Some of Allison's plans were pretty strange, and some of her costumes would have been impossible to make. But Colleen and the committee loved one idea: Everyone in the chorus was going to wear a special hat, this headgear with a long piece of coat-hanger wire sticking up from behind and looping out in front. A glittery star on a string would hang from the end of every wire. Then, as the chorus walked in, all the boys and girls would be following their own stars.

And Allison and the staging committee even came up with a special name for the concert. They wanted to call it "Winterhope."

Hart watched as Ross and two assistants spent those early days at sea carefully writing the names of holiday songs on the wide chalkboards at the front of the room. The list went on and on. Ross had made three big signs— PLEASE SAVE!—so the custodians wouldn't wash away their work at night.

The list of songs included old favorites like "Jingle Bells" and "White Christmas" and "Here Comes Santa Claus." There were Hanukkah songs like "I Have a Little Dreidel" and "Shalom, Children!" There were pop tunes like "Rockin' Around the Christmas Tree" and "Feliz Navidad," and traditional carols like "Silent Night" and "The First Noel."

And Heather Park and Jeanie Rhee had written some Korean words on the board. They wanted to sing a duet—a Korean Christmas carol.

After the third day Hart had said, "Hey, Ross—your list is getting pretty long."

Ross grinned proudly. "Yeah, isn't it great? Over eighty songs, and we're nowhere near done!"

Hart wanted to remind Ross that there would only be time for six, seven, maybe eight songs during the whole concert. But part of being a good captain is knowing what to say to the crew. So Hart gave Ross a slap on the shoulder and said, "Great job—*great* job!"

Hart smiled and nodded at Tim Miller as he started to pull his act together. Tim spent a lot of his time trying to figure out whether or not Elvis would wear a beard if he dressed up like Santa—some days it was yes, some days it was no.

Hart smiled and nodded at Mr. Meinert, too—whenever he happened to notice him. Most of the time Hart was too busy. But Mr. Meinert didn't feel left out now. He could see that Hart enjoyed being in charge, and he was fine with that. For now, Mr. Meinert was perfectly content to observe.

He watched as Captain Hart Evans set sail, watched as the voyage began. And just like Hart, Mr. Meinert enjoyed those first days at sea. He felt like an invisible stowaway. Whether Mr. Meinert sat at his desk or walked around the room, the kids usually ignored him. They didn't seem to care if he was listening or not. He got to see and hear everything, and he loved all the energy and enthusiasm. The room was never settled, but it was never completely crazy either.

These were new waters for him, too, and Mr. Meinert was paying attention. He was learning. And he felt like he was seeing real kids for the first time since he'd become a music teacher.

The memories of his first days as a student teacher were still fresh in his mind. He'd been thrown into a room with a huge gang of seventh graders. He had been a little too friendly, a little too timid, and the kids sensed that. They had refused to obey him. They went wild, and after fifteen minutes of chaos—fifteen minutes that had felt like ten hours—the regular music teacher had to rush back into the room and restore order. Mr. Meinert had been afraid of losing control of his classroom ever since.

That's why his classes had always been so carefully structured—especially the chorus. It was such a large group. Mr. Meinert had always planned every second of every class. He had directed all the activities, and he moved the kids from one task to the next with no breaks, no down time, no slack. He was able to accomplish a lot, but more importantly, he always had complete control.

The Chorus According to Hart didn't work like that. Was Hart in control? It didn't look like that way. Hart was steering the ship, sort of, but the rest of the kids, they were the ones who kept wind in the sails. And no matter how loud or fast the gale got blowing, Hart never seemed to be afraid.

Watching the kids had made Mr. Meinert reconsider his attitude about concerts, too. He had always believed that a school concert should be a polished little gem, a half hour of order and perfection, with no loose ends, nothing left to chance. And who was responsible for each and every detail? Simple: Mr. David Meinert, Chorus Director. The concerts had been *his* concerts. He had always felt the presence of his choral professor, or the principal, or the Director of Fine Arts from the high school. Out there in the audience, someone had always been watching *him*, judging *him*.

And in his own mind the big question had always been the same: How can I control this mob of twitchy kids and make them—*force* them—to put on this concert for me?

Hart Evans seemed to have a very different idea, if he actually had an idea at all. This thing that was coming on December 22—it wasn't going to be a concert. It was going to be more like an event.

Mr. Meinert hadn't forgotten his promise to Hart: *You can count on me*. Even though Hart hadn't asked for anything yet, Mr. Meinert knew he was already helping. He steadied the ship just by being the grown-up in the room. And Mr. Meinert had spoken with Mr. Richards about the student-run concert, and had found the principal to be surprisingly tolerant of the whole idea, even supportive. So the music teacher knew he was playing an important part in the process.

True, Hart had loads of natural talent. But after observing for seven class periods, Mr. Meinert felt pretty sure that sooner or later, Hart's call for help would come.

Fourteen

MUTINY

During those first seven class periods as the newly elected chorus director, Hart Evans had never felt so good about himself, about life in general, even about school. Everything was so much fun. Life was all yes, nothing but yes.

For one thing, Hart had reached a new level of popularity. Now he was known and admired by *all* the kids at Palmer Intermediate, not just the kids from his old elementary school. He was getting to be famous. He was doing something interesting. He was running the show in the chorus room, and for those first seven classes everyone had been having a blast. And why not? It was a huge, creative free-for-all. Do whatever you want to. Dream big. Ask Hart anything, and you know what he says? He says, "Great!" or, "Go for it!" or, "Sounds amazing!"

The news had spread. All over school the guys thought Hart was cool and the girls thought he was cute.

He was enjoying himself, but in the back of his mind Hart knew it couldn't go on like this. Everything was too fuzzy, too loose, always slightly out of focus. There were lots of ideas floating around and everyone was having fun, but the concert itself wasn't coming together. And the class periods kept ticking by.

Hart saw that part of his problem was human nature itself. Without a teacher to keep all the kids mixed together, the chorus had sorted itself into some basic personality types. And Hart had identified three groups: the doers, the floaters, and the goofers.

Some kids didn't fit neatly into those three main groups, so Hart also identified the floaty doers, the half-goofy floaters, and worst of all, the floaty goofers.

And then there was Tim Miller. Tim was a floaty goofy doer.

The serious goofers were mostly guys, and they had taken over the back corner of the room next to the windows. For them chorus had turned into goofer heaven. Three or four goofers played cards every day, someone always had a Hacky Sack in the air, and another one or two goofers just plugged into their CD players or iPods or Game Boys and zoned out for an hour. Goofers weren't productive, but they weren't disruptive, either.

The floaty goofers were a problem, but fortunately there were only two of them—Sara Boothe and Kyle Gannon. Sara and Kyle worked as a team, roaming around the room. Who changed those song names on the chalkboard into "Froggy the Snotman," "Jungle Smell Rock," and "The Little Dummer Boy?" Kyle and Sara. Who glued Colleen's backpack to the wall and put silver glitter in Ross's hair? Guess. At least once each period Mr. Meinert had to give Kyle and Sara the evil eye, and that helped. But floaty goofers need constant discipline, and The Chorus According to Hart wasn't set up that way.

The pure floaters and the floaty doers and the half-goofy floaters were fine as long as the doers kept them busy. Colleen was actually a superdoer, and she was also the biggest employer in the room. She had a crew of at least fifteen floaty types cutting out stars and streamers, and she kept them busy and focused all day, every day. Ross had two floaters and one floaty doer helping him get all the songs organized into groups, copied off the chalkboard, and neatly typed into Mr. Meinert's computer. There were also other doers like Allison Kim and Jim Barker, who had assembled small groups of floaters to help them with their projects. And then there were solo doers like the *Nutcracker* dancers and Carl Preston the magician who were busily organizing their own little events. Plus Lisa Morton, who was still working on a way to make herself fly around the stage like an angel.

After a hard look at the calendar at the beginning of the second week of December, Hart knew it was time to get serious. He had to start making decisions. It was time to take charge, time to get things organized. And it was certainly time to begin singing. Half the rehearsal days were gone, and the chorus hadn't sung a single note yet, at least not together, not as "the chorus."

So on Tuesday, December 7, Hart took his concert notes home. That night after dinner he looked at the long list of possible activities. He looked over Ross's list of recommended songs. And then Hart began being the director.

After an hour of thinking and rethinking, he turned on the computer in the family room and began to write, assembling the concert. Then he turned on the printer and made seventy-five copies.

And at the beginning of chorus period on December 8—with eleven rehearsal days to go—Hart called the chorus to order and passed out the programs.

"Hey!" yelled Tim Miller. "How come my name's not on the program?"

Carl shouted, "And what about my card trick?"

From the back of the room a girl called out, "Who said we wanted to sing 'The Little Drummer Boy'? That's such a stupid song!"

"Yeah," said Kyle, "'The Little Dummer Boy'!"

Colleen raised her hand, and Hart pointed at her, expecting a little support from his trusty lieutenant. But the pleasure cruise was over.

Colleen held up the program and said,

"Really, Hart, this looks like a regular old concert. We all walk onto the stage, we sing six songs, then we turn around and leave? I don't see anything special about this—and that was the whole idea, to make it special. I don't think—"

Hart shook his head. "Wait. . . wait. Let me explain. See, we don't just walk onstage. 'Cause this program, right now it's only a list of the songs, and there's stuff left out. Like, at the start, when we sing 'The Little Drummer Boy'? We have three drummers, me and Kenny and Tom, and we beat out the rhythm while everyone marches onto the stage singing the song. That's different. And maybe some kids could be carrying the big banner, 'Welcome to Winterhope.' And then 'Jingle Bells,' that'll be a sing-along, like karaoke, with the words on a screen so everyone in the audience can sing. Everybody loves that song. So that's different too. And during the dreidel song, Jenna and Max are going to be banging all over in those big rubbery costumes, even out in the audience. That'll be really funny. And when we sing 'The First Noel,' Shannon and Olivia can do some ballet stuff down in front, 'cause that'd look good, don't you think? So it's *not* just like a regular concert. There's tons of different stuff!"

Working it out in his mind the night before, the program had made perfect sense to Captain Hart. The crew didn't see it that way. Everyone burst out at once.

"These are the *worst* songs!"

"Yeah, and all that other stuff? It's so *lame*."

"I think the program stinks!"

"Yeah, me too! It's so . . . like, like, *boring*!"

"Yeah, it's *boring*!"

Carl Preston stood up and said, "How come I can't do my card trick? It's really good!"

Olivia Lambert said, "And I am not going to do *any* ballet dancing unless I can dance to my own music and be a Marzipan Shepherdess!"

Shannon Roda nodded and said, "Me either!"

Hart felt crushed. But also angry. He yelled, "Quiet! Everybody, quiet!" The room calmed down. "We're *not* having card tricks and ballet numbers and gymnastic routines. This is *not* a talent show, okay? It's a holiday concert, and we're the chorus. That's the whole idea. We can do different stuff, but we still have to sing—because . . . because we're the chorus."

Tim Miller jumped to his feet. "But I still get to be Elvis, right? Dressed up like Santa Claus?"

Hart nodded. "Yes. But you can't just bounce around onstage the whole time. You're gonna be out in front and do a lip sync when we sing the fifth number—that's 'Blue Christmas,' okay?"

Tim looked shocked. "No—no, that's not it! I'm gonna be, like, all over the place all the time, you know, like a clown at the circus. I'm gonna be *so* funny—like really, really funny!" And grabbing his air guitar, Tim swiveled over to Melanie Enson, put his cheek down close to her face, and in his best Tennessee accent said, "How'd you like to give Elvis a big ol' kiss?"

That got some kids laughing, but most of the chorus was still upset with the program, and after a couple more loud complaints, Hart had had enough.

"Listen," he said. "I'm the director, and for now, this is the concert. So deal with it. We've only got eleven days, only *eleven* days! And we have to get it all pulled together. And we have to rehearse the songs. And everything else, too. So . . . let's just do it. We *have* to do it!"

Ed Farley, the king of the goofers, shouted out, "How come we have to do it?" and three or four other kids yelled, "Yeah, how come?"

Hart Evans pulled himself up to his full height and glared at Ed, cold fury crackling in his eyes. Then Hart shouted something he had never said before—something he could never have imagined himself saying, not in a million years. "How come?" he yelled. *"Because* I *said so!* That's how come! Now let's get to work! Boys, over on this side of the room. Girls, over there. Ross, pass out the sheets with the words to 'The Little Drummer Boy.' NOW!"

And the kids obeyed him.

When everyone was in place, Hart turned and said, "Mr. Meinert, I need you to play the piano."

For the next thirty-five minutes Hart stood at the front of the room pointing first at the boys, and then at the girls as the chorus rehearsed "The Little Drummer Boy." Hart had Kenny playing along on a snare drum. It didn't sound bad, but it wasn't great, either.

The period ended, and the kids began to gather up their things. There was no laughing, no chatter as the room emptied. No one looked at Hart, no one went near him.

Walking out of the room, Hart was right behind Shannon Roda. In the most cheerful voice he could manage, Hart said, "Hey, Shannon, that went okay, don't you think?"

She stopped in the doorway and turned to look at him. So did Olivia.

Shannon said, "Are you talking to *me*? Because, *don't*. You're just like Mr. Meinert. Only shorter. And meaner. You know what you are?" Shannon narrowed her green eyes and hissed. "You're a *teacher*!"

Fifteen

DEEP WATERS

Another beautiful day. Cold, but bright and sunny. Perfect December day, don't you think?"

Hart nodded at his dad, and he tried to smile a little, tried to act like he cared about the weather. But he didn't. It was only seven fifteen on Thursday morning, and Hart was already thinking about chorus, about the concert, about what a huge mess it was. It was all he could think about, all day every day, all night every night.

Staring down at the blue-and-white plate, Hart took another bite of toast.

Hart's mom caught her husband's eye, and then nodded toward their son, raising her eyebrows. The look said, "Go on, keep talking. Can't you see he needs help?" Because it was clear to everyone in the family that Hart was going through some deep waters.

Even Sarah knew something was up. Two

days ago Hart had come into his room after school and caught her there, back at his work-bench in the corner. She was sitting in his chair, actually holding Hart's small high-speed electric drill in her hand.

"*Hey!* What're you doing in here?"

That part had been pretty normal, when Hart shouted at her.

Sarah gulped and held out her left hand. "I . . . I want to make a hole in this shell I found in Florida. I want to put it on a chain, like a neck-lace."

It was the next part that had tipped her off. Because instead of yelling some more and grabbing her arm and pushing her out of his room, Hart had said, "Well, be careful. That's a diamond drill bit on that thing, and it'll go right through your finger."

Then Hart had just flopped onto his bed, pulled a clipboard and a pencil out of his back-pack, and started writing.

The evidence was clear to Sarah: Something was definitely weird in Hartsville.

His mom had begun to notice it right after Thanksgiving. Little things at first, like forgetting to stay after school and sign up for winter indoor soccer league. And spending more time on the phone, sometimes getting two or three phone calls a night from boys she'd never heard of—and girls, too. And why was he singing that "Little Drummer Boy" song in the shower every morning? Even more puzzling, after all Hart had said about the new computer games he was hoping for, she had had to ask him three times to make a Christmas list.

Hart's dad took a sip of orange juice and then said, "So Hart, how about a ride to school today? We can leave early and take the long way, even take a spin out onto the Parkway if the traffic's not too bad. How about it?"

That got Hart's attention. The little silver sports car was not to be ignored, no matter what. "Yeah, that'd be great."

"Five minutes?"

Hart nodded. "I'll be ready," and he was—a full two minutes early, with book bag stowed in the trunk and seat belt tight across his chest.

His dad backed out of the driveway, put the car in first gear, and said, "Hold on." He punched the gas and—zip—the car jumped to forty miles an hour in about a second and a half, pushing Hart straight back into the tan leather seat.

He grinned over at his dad and said, "Sweet!"

The car had some serious sizzle, and Hart loved the way the thing hugged the ground as they shot around the corner onto Oak Road. His dad kept the car right at the speed limit, cruising along on the winding back roads for about ten miles. Then he had to slow down when he turned onto a busy highway that led out toward the Parkway.

His dad pushed a button and the small screen in the center of the dashboard lit up. At another tap, the screen showed a map, a grid of streets and highways, and it was littered with blinking red octagons. "That's the GPS traffic advisory screen. See those little stop signs?" his dad asked.

Hart nodded.

"Those are traffic delays. We'd better not try the Parkway. So I'm going to turn around up there at the circle and head back the way we came."

As they worked their way through the crowded intersection, Hart kept craning his neck to see the drivers of the other cars, checking out the passengers, too, watching to see the looks on their faces when they saw how amazing his dad's car was. And people did notice.

Hart grinned. "Don't you love how everybody looks at you when you drive around in this car? It's like they can't help it."

His dad gave a short laugh. "I almost didn't get this car for that very reason."

Hart turned to look at his dad. "No way!"

"I'm serious. I could care less what anybody else thinks about me, or this car, or me driving around in this car. That's not why I bought it."

As they stopped at a red light, Hart nodded at a teenage boy driving a small pickup. He had two of his friends squeezed into the small cab with him.

"See the kid in the truck next to us, the guy in the Yankees cap? He's been staring at this car for two minutes, talking to his buddies about it, just *wishing* he could take it for a drive. And you don't think that's cool?"

His dad smiled and shrugged. "No, because I really don't care. I'm not *trying* to make people envy me. I just want to drive a beautifully engineered automobile. This car—it's like driving a Swiss watch: Everything works perfectly, everything does exactly what it's supposed to with no wasted energy, no wasted motion, and all that power under perfect control. It's just a great machine. And that's all I care about. Honestly. "

Hart was quiet as his dad put the car through its paces again along the back roads, headed toward school.

After a few minutes his dad said, "You haven't seemed much like yourself in the past week or so, Hart. Something been bothering you?"

Hart shook his head. "Nah. Just school stuff. Bunch of kids are kind of mad at me."

"Angry? At you? What about?"

"Just some stupid stuff. In chorus. There's a concert, and I'm sort of in charge of it, and it's like I can't do anything right. Everybody wants to do stuff their way."

"How come you're in charge? What about

the teacher . . . Mr. What's-his-name?"

"Meinert. Mr. Meinert. He's there too, but I'm supposed to get the thing organized."

"Ah, so you're the boss."

Hart gave a sarcastic little snort. "You could say that. Except nobody does what I tell them to."

It was quiet for another mile or so. Then Hart's dad said, "I've had a little experience at being a boss, you know. It's not easy. Because you can't just give orders. I spend a lot of my time listening. People aren't going to do something—I mean, they won't do it *well*—unless they really want to."

Hart looked out the window, watching the leafless woods fly by, a gray and brown blur.

As the car swung into the circle at the front of the school, his dad said, "It'll all work out, Hart. You're a good boss, a good leader. Kids look up to you—they always have. Something'll open up. Try listening a little more. That's what always helps me."

He was about to reply to his dad, but when they came to a stop right in front of the main doors, Hart had a memory burst. He sat up straight as it jolted into his mind. He knew this moment! He had run this scene in his mind a dozen times. This was his big school drop-off scene, the moment to emerge from the very cool car, just the way he had imagined it.

As his dad pulled the lever to pop open the trunk, Hart glanced around to check out his audience.

The buses hadn't arrived, so the front of the school was practically deserted. Pretty disappointing. But about thirty feet away four girls stood waiting near bus stop number two. It wasn't exactly the admiring crowd Hart had pictured, but the flashy car had definitely caught the girls' attention. So Hart decided to make the most of it.

Hart could tell that all four heads turned as he made a smooth exit from the car, stepped to the trunk and pulled out his backpack.

He walked back to the open door, leaned down and smiled at his dad. "Thanks for the ride. And for what you said."

His dad smiled back. "You have a great day, all right? See you tonight."

Hart pushed the door shut, and just as he'd

imagined it, the little bullet car purred away from the curb, blinked, turned left, and then sped off down Highway 12.

And now it was time to see the girls smile, perhaps nod or wave, maybe even hurry over and say, "Is that your dad's car? It's so *cool*!"

Hart pivoted slowly, a generous smile on his face.

The girls stood there. They glared at Hart a moment, and then, in almost perfect unison, they turned their backs and walked away.

And as they did, Hart knew why.

They were all members of the sixth grade chorus.

Sixteen

RESCUE

On Thursday afternoon Carl Preston met Hart in the doorway of the chorus room, a copy of the concert program in one hand, a deck of cards in the other. He shook the paper and said, "This is wrong, Hart, can't you see that? And it's not what Ross said. Ross said I could be in the show. He said I could have seven minutes, and look—I'm not even on the program! It's a *great* card trick, you should see it, Hart. C'mon, let me show it to you."

Hart shook his head. "Seven minutes is way too long. That's like one-fifth of the whole time, Carl. Besides, I still don't get why Ross told you this could be part of the concert at all. And he said you want to wear your magician costume? It just doesn't fit . . . can't you see that? It's supposed to be a *concert*. Listen, we'll talk about this later, okay?"

Carl hurried to keep up as Hart kept walking. "But Hart, you should see—it's such a great trick, and I learned it from my grampa, and he's gonna be at the concert. He'd love it! Maybe I could dress up like one of the three wise men, you know, from the Christmas story? They were sort of like magicians, right?"

Hart waved Carl off and walked down front to the chalkboard. He erased the number *eleven* and replaced it with the number *ten*, about six inches tall.

Ten. That's how many class periods were left before the concert. Hart turned and watched the rest of the kids straggle into the chorus room.

Turning back to the board, Hart looked again. Still ten—a one and a zero.

Hart could see what was coming. He could see it clearly now. Ten more class periods to prepare—only ten—and then . . . complete disaster.

Hart Evans had been getting the cold shoulder all day. It was a new experience for him, and Hart didn't like it.

After the scene with the girls out front in the morning, he had walked up to a bunch of his buddies before school. Everyone stopped talking and scattered.

When he had walked through the halls between morning classes, no one smiled, no one said hello.

When Hart went to his usual lunch table, it was empty, and it stayed that way until Alex had dropped into the seat across from him.

Alex glanced around and said, "Where is everybody?"

Hart smirked. "Haven't you heard? About me and the chorus? I've become an outcast."

Alex was in the orchestra. "Oh, that. Yeah, I heard." He shrugged. "So what do you care about what a bunch of idiots think? Somebody's got to be in charge. And if there are jerks around—and there are *always* jerks around—somebody's got to tell them to shut up and get to work."

Hart smiled, and what Alex said made him feel a little better. But he still had some trouble swallowing his grilled cheese sandwich.

After lunch Hart had waved across the cafeteria to Zack. Zack turned his back and began to walk away. Hart hurried and caught up with him in the gym. He grabbed Zack's backpack and spun him around. "Hey! I wave and you walk away? What's your problem?"

Zack said, "*My* problem? What, are you dumb? Don't you know what you shouted at Ed in chorus yesterday? I mean, it's all over the school. You said he had to sing some stupid song, and he said how come, and you said, 'Because I said so!' You *said* that. To another kid. That's like, so *wrong*. Kids don't say that. Only moms and dads say that. And teachers. Catch you later."

And Zack was gone.

A lot of kids go through school without being very popular, mostly because no one knows who they are. They pass unnoticed, unchallenged. Hart wasn't simply unknown now. He was known and actively disliked. In less than twenty-four hours, the most popular boy at Palmer Intermediate School had become the least popular.

And that's why, twenty minutes later, standing at the front of the chorus room with that big number ten on the chalkboard behind him, Hart Evans had never felt so alone.

The bell rang, and as the echo faded Mr. Meinert walked in from the hall with a huge smile on his face. He called down to the front of the room, "Hey Hart, it looks like a go!" And he gave Hart a big thumbs-up.

Hart had no clue what Mr. Meinert was talking about. He smiled and nodded anyway.

Mr. Meinert hurried through the jumble of folding desks. Looking around at the class, he said, "I checked something out for Hart, and it looks like it'll be okay. The old gym is available for the chorus to use. Mr. Richards says he'll pull some strings for us. That way the chorus can put on its own separate event. There's the stage at one end if you want to use it, and there'll be plenty of room for just about anything. And the custodians said they'll set up the folding chairs any way you want. Plus there are the old bleachers on both sides. We can even get in there and set up three or four days before the concert. Then on the night of the concert, the band and orchestra will perform first in the auditorium, and after intermission everyone will walk over to the old gym for the chorus program. So it's all going to work out. Such a great idea!"

Looking at Hart, Colleen said, "You mean

we can get in there and put up our decorations, and no one will even see them before the concert?"

Going with the flow, Hart nodded.

Colleen said, "That'll be *great*!"

Olivia jumped to her feet. "Does this mean there'll be room for our ballet dancing?"

Hart gulped. "Um . . . I don't really know. . . yet." Which was true.

Hart's mind was racing now, trying to understand what Mr. Meinert had said, trying to understand how a concert in the old gym might work, trying to figure out what to say and do next.

But thinking on his feet was one of Hart's best talents, so he gulped again and just started talking, giving his mind a chance to catch up, "Well . . . um . . . after yesterday, I started thinking . . . and what I was thinking . . . was . . . well . . ."

And then, like a sudden puff of wind across calm waters, Hart got an idea. "I was thinking . . . that we should go back . . . like to the beginning. Because at the beginning there was an election. And everybody elected me to be the director—

which was pretty crazy. But it solved the problem . . . sort of. Except now everybody's got a million ideas about what the concert should be like . . . and that's a new problem . . . like, which ideas to pick. And it's a lot of pressure. On me."

Then came a stroke of genius. Hart looked toward the back of the room and nodded at Ed Farley. "And I'm sorry I sounded like such a jerk yesterday."

Hart paused long enough for Ed to give him a half smile and a shrug, and then he went on. "So I say we should all vote, about everything—like which songs to sing. . . what the whole concert should be like, which kids will do stuff. We vote about everything. But first we have to agree that no matter which songs or ideas win, everybody's got to go along with the winners—the whole chorus. Okay? Anybody want to say anything else?"

Kids began sifting the idea, and the room buzzed—some positive noise, some negative. Even the goofers in the back corner were paying attention.

Ross raised his hand. "I think I know how

the voting should work. It's like Student Council elections. First come nominations— for songs or different parts of the concert. Then we make a ballot with all the nominated songs and everything. After the ballots are set, kids get to talk about which stuff they think should win—that's the campaigning. And then every kid gets to vote, but only for six different things. And then the seven or eight things with the most votes win. Because the whole concert can only be about thirty-five minutes long."

Hart waited for someone else to say something, but when no one did, he said, "That sounds good to me." And then he pointed over his shoulder at the big number he'd written on the chalkboard. "But there are only ten rehearsal periods left, so we have to do this fast—like today. Does what Ross said sound good to you guys? Show of hands for yes."

Almost every hand went up.

Hart said, "Okay. Then let's get started."

The rest of the period was democracy's finest hour. The nominations came thick and fast, all mixed together—for songs, for special acts, for solo performances—and Mr. Meinert sat at his computer table, typing everything onto a ballot. After about twenty minutes everyone agreed there were enough nominations, and Mr. Meinert printed out one ballot for each kid.

Then the room was opened up for campaigning.

Allie Marston stood up and said, "We just *have* to sing 'Silent Night.' I think it's the best song, because . . . it's really about Christmas."

James Archer said, "Yeah, but what about where it says 'the Savior is born' and stuff—maybe kids from other religions don't want to sing that."

Jenna said, "I'm Jewish, and I don't care. I think my parents might, but not me. It's only a song. It's not like we're trying to change anybody's religion. If somebody gets mad we can say it's just educational, learning about other religions. And we can include something about Islam. And Kwanzaa, too. But what I really wanted to say is that I hope we can sing the dreidel song—mostly because it's fast and funny."

Carl made a pitch for his card trick, Shannon

and Olivia talked up their ballet number, and Heather and Jeanie said they still wanted to sing a Korean Christmas carol.

Ann said, "What about the karaoke idea, where we make people come up from the audience and sing along with the chorus? I still like that idea."

Lots of kids made little speeches about their favorite songs, and right near the end Hart said, "And I still think we should do 'The Little Drummer Boy'—because the drumming stuff could be cool."

With about five minutes left in the period, Hart said, "Okay. Time to vote. Everyone pick six things you want to be in the program. I'll come in after school and count, and Mr. Meinert will check everything. Then tomorrow we can see the results and start rehearsing. So everybody mark your ballots now."

The room hushed—only crinkling paper and the scratching of pencils and pens.

Tim Miller called out, "If I mess up and want to change something, can I just cross it out? 'Cause I'm using a pen."

Hart nodded, and the voting continued.

When the bell rang, Hart hurried toward the doorway, and said, "Give me your ballots on the way out."

Tim Miller shouted, "Me first!" and rushed over to cast his ballot. He had folded his paper into a tiny square lump, and on one side in red marker it said TOP SECRET.

Hart called out, "And please, only fold your ballot once."

On his way through the door Ross said, "Good idea, Hart."

Hart said, "Thanks. Yours too."

Ed Farley handed over his ballot, and in a voice low enough so only Hart could hear, he said, "If 'Drummer Boy' makes it, think I could play too? I had a couple lessons."

"Sure," Hart nodded. "Why not?"

And as a crowd of girls hurried out, Hart even got half a smile from Shannon Roda.

When the room was empty, Hart carried the stack of ballots down to the front of the room. "Mr. Meinert, where should I put these?"

"Over here. I've got a big envelope."

Hart handed him the ballots. Then he said, "At the beginning of the period? How come you acted like moving the concert to the gym was my idea?"

Mr. Meinert smiled and said, "How come you didn't stop me and tell everyone that you had nothing to do with it?"

Hart grinned. "Because I was dead meat, that's how come. I needed all the help I could get."

Still smiling, Mr. Meinert nodded. "Exactly."

"Well, it worked great," said Hart. "So thanks. A lot."

"You're welcome."

Mr. Meinert paused a moment, and then said, "But next time you need help, remember to ask. I said you could count on me, and I meant it."

Hart nodded. "Okay. I'll remember." He picked up his backpack and started toward the door.

Then he stopped and said, "How'd you come up with that idea—moving to the old gym?"

It was Mr. Meinert's turn to grin. "Simple. I've been learning a lot this past couple weeks. So I just asked myself, 'If I was as crazy as Hart Evans, what would I do next?'"

Hart laughed. "Right. So I'll see you after school . . . to count," and he hurried out to get to his next class.

Mr. Meinert sat at his desk and opened the big drawer. From a file labeled LARGE ENVELOPES he pulled one out and began stuffing the ballots into it, slowly shaking his head, a smile still on his face.

A few short weeks ago he had hoped Hart Evans would fall flat on his face. He had wanted the kid to hand the concert back, sit down, and shut up. Earlier today as he had talked with the principal, and then with the gym teachers and the custodians, Mr. Meinert had realized how important this concert had become to him. He wanted it to be a success.

None of this was about him—Mr. Meinert could see that now. In two weeks, this wouldn't even be his school anymore. But after those two weeks, the kids—including Hart Evans— they would still be *his* students.

And this concert was *their* concert.

Seventeen

ACCOUNTING

On Friday, December 10—countdown day number nine—Hart delivered the election results to the rest of the voters.

The thirty-six nominated songs and activities had faced the popular vote. Democracy itself had worked perfectly. So democracy wasn't the problem.

The problem was math.

With seventy-four kids casting 6 votes each, there had been a total of 444 votes. If each of the thirty-six different ballot choices had been equally popular, then they would have gotten an equal number of votes—a little more than 12 votes each. But, of course, it hadn't worked that way.

The three biggest winners—"Frosty the Snowman," "Deck the Halls," and "O Little Town of Bethlehem"—had been extremely popular, and all together had taken 181 votes.

The next three winners—"Jingle Bells," "I

Have a Little Dreidel," and "We Wish You a Merry Christmas"—had been quite popular too, taking another 96 votes. So after the top six items had drawn 277 votes, the thirty other possible choices were left to split up the remaining votes: 167.

If each of the thirty remaining ballot choices had been equally popular, then each would have gotten between 5 and 6 votes—and this is the interesting part: Most of them did. And since most of them did, that meant that the last two highest vote getters didn't have to get very many votes to win—one got only 11 votes and one got just 9 votes. And the last two winners were the *Nutcracker* ballet number and Carl Preston's card trick.

There was nothing to argue about. Democracy had run its course and the numbers told the truth. But numbers don't account for feelings.

Carl Preston, and Shannon and Olivia, and the friends who had voted for them were happy—so about fifteen kids were thrilled with the results.

The rest of the kids in the chorus weren't sure how they felt.

Except for Tom Denby. He was sure. He stood up and said, "I move that we have another election. Nobody wants to see some lame card trick. What Hart said yesterday, about this not being a talent show? That's right. And that stupid dancing? That stuff makes me gag. So I say we vote again!"

Shannon spun around in her desk. "Only *idiots* don't like ballet! So let's take a vote on that. Everyone who thinks Tommy's an idiot raise your hand and say 'Idiot'!"

A dozen girls waved their arms and screeched, "*Idiot!*"

The room exploded like a grease fire.

The girls began chanting, "Id-i-ot! Id-i-ot! Id-i-ot!"

"Nuh-uh—you're the idiots! And even if you had talent, ballet would still rot!"

"Id-i-ot! Id-i-ot! Id-i-ot!"

Almost having to shout, Allison said, "Do we really want to have a card trick? As part of the concert? A *card trick*?"

"I'm with you," called Ed. "Card tricks are for losers!"

"Says who!" That was Carl.

"Says me!"

"Oh, yeah?"

"Yeah!"

"Shut up!"

"Make me!"

"Shut up!"

"No, you shut up!"

"Id-i-ot! Id-i-ot! Id-i-ot!"

"Shut up!"

And above the snapping flames, Tim Miller was trying to get Hart's attention. "Hart! Elvis is still in the show, right? Hey, Hart! Hart! Elvis? Elvis is okay, right? Right? Hart? *Hart!*"

Hart was paralyzed. The election had been completely fair. And now this. Anything he said would only make people angrier. The noise in the room made it impossible to think.

Hart looked over at Mr. Meinert and . . . he couldn't believe it. The guy was sitting on his desk, calmly looking out at the madness in his classroom. It seemed like he didn't have a care in the world. Hart even thought he saw a slight smile.

Mr. Meinert turned and caught Hart's glance. The teacher smiled and shrugged.

Hart did not see the humor in the situation. Mr. Meinert saw that, and immediately adjusted the expression on his face.

Hart kept looking at him. And then Hart raised his eyebrows and moved his lips, forming a silent word.

And Mr. Meinert got the message.

The word was, *Help!*

Eighteen

JUST AN IDEA

Mr. Meinert got up and walked over until he stood in front of Hart, almost bumping up against the kids sitting in the first row of folding desks. He raised one hand over his head and waited.

Mr. Meinert doing anything was unusual these days, so everyone noticed him right away. In less than fifteen seconds all the shouting stopped and the kids settled into their desks.

Bringing his hand down, Mr. Meinert said, "Thanks. I just wanted to ask a question. Where did the name 'Winterhope' come from?"

Colleen raised her hand. Mr. Meinert pointed and she said, "From Allison. She made it up. Because when *Cirque du Soleil* makes a new show, they always give it a special name. So that's what Allison did. And we all liked it and decided to call the concert Winterhope."

"But the name itself," said Mr. Meinert. "What does it mean? Winterhope—hope for what?"

Allison raised her hand and said, "For peace. That's what I was thinking. A holiday concert could be about hoping for peace. And the holidays always come in the winter. So, Winterhope."

Mr. Meinert wrote P-E-A-C-E on the chalkboard in big letters. Then he stood back and pointed at it. "You know what that is? It's a theme, one big idea. If you have a theme you can build a program around it. You've all had so many good ideas over these last few weeks. And voting to solve your problems? Just great. But if you want to pull a program together, you might want to think about Allison's idea of peace. That could really help. Anybody else have a thought about this?"

Carl raised his hand and said, "So what you're really saying is, I can't do my card trick, right?"

Mr. Meinert shook his head. "I'm not saying that at all. And it's not my concert. It's up to all of you. I'm just asking if anyone else thinks

Allison's idea could be a theme. You've all come up with so many creative ideas. I hate to see any of them not get used—except that's probably impossible. But with a theme like peace, a concert could tell a story. Maybe about the search for peace. Or about the need for peace. About the kinds of things people have time for when they're not fighting and killing each other. Like ballet and magic acts. And maybe a concert with a theme could use more of your ideas. That's all I'm saying."

Less than a month ago, before The Chorus According to Hart, Mr. Meinert would have kept going. He would have started barking orders, giving directions, getting things organized, pushing a plan forward. Not today. He looked around at all the faces in the quiet room and said, "It's just an idea." Then he walked back over to his desk and sat down.

It was exactly the right amount of help, and the right kind, too.

Hart got it.

Peace. The theme was a like a lens, and in Hart's mind ideas began snapping into focus. Before the room got noisy again, Hart said,

"Allison's idea is great, don't you think? I mean, we can do a million things with that! Don't you think?"

Hart wasn't the only one who got it. Heads were nodding all around the room. Carolyn raised her hand and said, "How about if we had a narrator, sort of telling a story, like Mr. Meinert said. We've read plays like that in drama club sometimes."

Ross said, "We'd have to write all that out, so someone could read it—the narration, I mean."

"Right," said Hart, "only it doesn't have to be real long. But it's going to take some work. Still, I think it's a good idea, don't you? Anybody here who's not in favor of peace?"

Olivia raised her hand. Hart knew what was coming, and he was ready.

She said, "What about the election yesterday? Was all that just a joke?"

Hart shook his head. "No. That election was fair and square. So all the things that won have to be part of the concert now . . . unless we *all* decide otherwise. We just have to figure out a way to make everything work together. And . . .

and that's the whole idea of peace, anyway, to make everything get along together. With no fighting."

Mr. Meinert felt the mood of the room begin to change. It was like a midwinter thaw, a warm front sweeping across the group, one kid at a time.

Hart felt it too, and he kept talking. "I know we can do this. And peace is a huge idea. It's really important. We all have to think and work together until we figure it out. For the concert. We can do this. We really can."

Everyone bought in. The kids didn't just believe Hart. They trusted him. And they also trusted themselves.

Nineteen

CRUNCH TIME

The earth kept turning, and every time it did, December 22 got one day closer. Hart kept one eye on the calendar, and the other on the frantic preparations.

Anyone else observing the chorus during those last eleven days would have had a tough time guessing the theme of the concert. Not one of the remaining class periods, not one of the hours before and after school spent working on decorations, not one of the long weekend sessions practicing new songs and preparing the old gym—nothing even remotely resembled peace.

It took real work to keep the theme in view. To Hart, those eleven days often looked more like a major military operation—and sometimes it was all out war.

There were battles about which songs worked with the theme and which ones didn't. There was open conflict about which nonmusical events could be included, and once that was settled, there were heated disputes about the order of the program.

There were clashes about who should write the narration, and then disagreement about what the narration should be, followed by controversies over who should read which parts. Alliances and coalitions developed, ruled the world for a day or so, and then splintered into rival factions and collapsed. There were tussles and scuffles, quarrels and spats, tiffs and squabbles.

The road to peace wasn't easy. But thankfully, all the conflict happened within the framework of a fragile, but miraculously effective, sixth grade democracy.

And amid the wrangling and bickering, Hart also saw progress, hour by hour, day by day.

School concerts rarely happen without help from parents. This one was no exception, and when the parent brigade began to work side by side with the kids, Hart felt certain for the first time that this concert was actually going to happen. True, it might still end up being a huge embarrassment, but it was definitely going to happen.

At least a dozen moms and dads began helping Colleen and her decorating crew, some directly, and some just donating materials. Cardboard and Styrofoam and paint and glue and glitter and string and wire began to pile up so much that the whole decorating operation had to be moved from the chorus room to the stage in the old gym.

One mom brought a portable sewing machine and stitched three king-size sheets together. Under Allison's direction three other parents helped a group of kids paint the huge banner. Then they began working on several smaller banners and signs.

On the Sunday before the Wednesday concert, six moms and four dads showed up to help hang the decorations and adjust the sound system and set up the folding chairs in the pattern that Jim Barker had designed. There weren't going to be any raised platforms, and the lighting wasn't going to remind anyone of a TV show, but Jim had presented some creative ideas, and the chorus had voted and approved.

Lisa Morton's dad had decided not to spend twelve thousand dollars on wiring and harnesses so his little girl could fly like an angel, but he and Lisa had come up with something else almost as dramatic. And on that last Sunday afternoon they were both hard at work in the old gym.

Mr. Meinert kept to the background, but he was hard at work too. He was the one convincing the P. E. teachers to double up their classes and stay out of the old gym for a few days. He was the one convincing teachers with lunch duty to take the kids to the playground instead of the old gym on these blustery December days. He was the one assuring the principal that he hadn't lost his mind and that he wasn't trying to give the school a black eye by letting sixth graders run their own concert. He was the one showing up at school early, and working with the soloists during his lunch period, and staying late almost every evening. He was the one making sure the doors of the old gym were open on Saturday morning and Sunday afternoon, and then locked again after everyone else had gone home.

Mr. Meinert was the one who also had to try to find some peace in his own home. The extra time he spent at school was not helping him find a new job. His wife was not happy about the long hours, and Lucy Meinert had plenty to say about it.

"You told me that you'd thrown this whole holiday concert mess back at those ungrateful kids, and what did I do? I applauded. I praised you. I thought, 'My wonderful husband is finally getting smart. He's finally getting fed up with the way that miserable school system has been treating him.' And now this. Honestly, David. You know what? It's a good thing you're getting fired, that's what. Because if you weren't, I don't know if I could just stand by and watch someone I love struggle so hard to keep on teaching when he knows his whole career is swirling away down the drain!"

And Mr. Meinert was the one patiently playing the piano, accompanying the chorus every class period as they scrambled to learn a bunch of new songs in far too little time. At Hart's invitation, he had offered suggestions about songs that might work with their theme, and he'd made some suggestions about the very last song, too. But once the chorus had made their choices, he was just the accompanist. That was the hardest part for him. He wanted to begin giving orders. He wanted to make the kids learn their harmony parts. It wasn't going to happen. He faced the fact that almost all the singing would be in unison—the way first graders usually sound.

As the chorus destroyed pronunciations and slurred words together and slid from note to note instead of making crisp transitions, he ignored his years of musical training. He kept his yearning for choral perfection to himself. He stayed focused on the fact that with very little help from him or anyone else, these kids were creating something unique—maybe even wonderful. Well . . . *wonderful* was probably too much to expect.

But regardless, Mr. Meinert looked forward to Wednesday night the way a parent looks forward to seeing a child take those first few steps alone—alone, but not really.

Twenty

PEACE

On the evening of December 22, Palmer Intermediate School was packed. More than four hundred parents and teachers and relatives had come to the holiday concert.

Beginning promptly at 7 PM, the sixth grade band performed their selections well, and the applause rang out long and loud.

The sixth grade orchestra struggled a bit with Mozart, and then had a real wrestling match with Beethoven. But in the end, it was good music and good education, and again, applause filled the auditorium.

Following the instructions on their program sheets, the crowd went to the cafeteria, enjoyed their intermission refreshments, and then began following the signs leading to the old gym. Some of the families with younger children went home after intermission, and some families with no kids singing in the chorus left too. But more than three hundred people found their way to the second half of the concert.

The sixth grade chorus was ready.

A corner of the area outside the gym had been decorated to look like a U.S.O. hall, a place soldiers can visit when they're away from home. There were red, white, and blue streamers all over, and big banners.

PEACE! PEACE!

THE WARS ARE OVER!

EVERYONE IS GOING HOME FOR THE HOLIDAYS!

FREE SHOW TONIGHT!

A small stage made out of risers had been set up in the corner, and a group of kids from the chorus—including Ed Farley and three other goofers—were dressed up like soldiers, standing there watching the show. And the show was Carl Preston, in his full magician's costume. During the intermission he performed his card trick plus four of his best magic routines. The little kids loved it, and so did Carl's grandfather.

As the crowd worked its way past the show in the foyer and entered the gym, people took their seats quietly. It would have been rude to talk, because on the stage at the end of the gym, Shannon and Olivia were performing the Dance of the Marzipan Shepherdesses. The lights above the stage threw a reddish glow onto the girls as they danced. The music was bright and festive, but peaceful, which was the idea. And even Tom Denby would have had to admit that the girls looked graceful— and talented. Beautiful, too. The dance was only about three minutes long, so they performed the entire dance four times before the whole audience had arrived, and then they bowed for their applause.

When the hallway was empty and the ballerinas had taken their final bows, the curtain closed and the lights began to dim. The old gym fell into darkness, lit only by the faint red glow of the EXIT signs.

From far away, out in the echoing hallway, a deep bell rang—*dong, dong, dong*—and the audience hushed, straining to hear the distant sound.

As the bell in the hall kept ringing, another one with a different tone began to toll from behind the curtains on the stage. And then a third bell began to chime from the far corner of the long room, way up on the bleachers near the ceiling. A fourth bell, hidden in a utility closet along the east wall of the gym, added its voice.

The bells got softer, and the curtain opened. Hundreds of glittering stars seemed to hang in midair above the children onstage. The sixth grade chorus took three steps forward, waited for one chord from the piano, and then began to sing.

> "I heard the bells on Christmas day,
> Their old familiar carols play.
> And wild and sweet the words repeat,
> of peace on earth, good will to men."

The chorus continued humming the tune, and a single spotlight swung toward the side of the stage and focused on Carolyn Payton. She read from a paper, squinting into the brightness as she stepped to the microphone.

> "This year the chorus got to choose its own songs and make its own decorations and come up with its own ideas.

And we chose one simple idea as the theme of our concert, a very important idea: Peace.

"The holidays are a time for traditions. Some holiday traditions go back thousands of years, like Christmas and Hanukkah and Ramadan. Some holiday traditions are newer, like Thanksgiving and Kwanzaa.

"But old or new, all over the world, holiday traditions bring us closer to our beliefs and closer to our families. Holidays remind us that every family wants to live and worship in freedom and peace.

"Peace. That is what families everywhere hope for. And that is why our chorus program has a special name this year."

As the huge banner unrolled above the front of the stage, Carolyn said,

"Welcome . . . to 'Winterhope'!"

The piano hit a chord, the chorus split left and right, and in the brightly lit center of the stage, four tall panels of cardboard rose up from the floor—a Christmas tree painted on one, a gold menorah on the second, a silver crescent on the third, and a black, red, and green kinara on the fourth.

"We wish you a Happy Holidays!
We wish you a Happy Holidays!
We wish you a Happy Holidays,
And a Happy New Year!

Good tidings we bring,
to you and your kin.
Good tidings for the holidays,
And a Happy New Year!"

Applause burst out, and as it died down, Ross stepped to the microphone.

"If there was no hope for peace, would we walk around saying, 'Happy Holidays' to each other? And without peace, would there be any happy songs at all?

"What if 'Jingle Bells' had been written in a time of war?

The lights faded to a murky blue, and the chorus limped slowly around the stage, moaning the words while Mr. Meinert played the tune in a minor key.

> *"Things are bad, things are bad,*
> *Nothing makes me glad.*
> *All the news is scary,*
> *and I don't know where my dad is.*
> *I'm so sad, I'm so sad,*
> *I don't want to play.*
> *If the war was over*
> *I would have a better day."*

The spotlight came up on Ross again.

"But the song was written in a time of peace, and it's filled with fun. So here's the real 'Jingle Bells,' and it's a sing-along!"

The words of the song flashed onto a screen on the wall beside the stage, and as hundreds of people began to sing, the side doors opened, and into the gym burst a one-horse open sleigh—a child's wagon transformed by cardboard and paint. Tom Denby wore a plastic horse's head and a tail made of frayed rope. He trotted up and down the aisles in rhythm to the music, pulling the sleigh and whinnying at random intervals.

And riding in the sleigh was none other than Tim Miller dressed up as Elvis who was dressed up as Santa. Without a beard. Elvis swung his hips and sang at the top of his lungs, simultaneously blasting metallic twangs from a real electric guitar and a portable amplifier that was hooked onto the wagon with bungee cords. Tim as Elvis as Santa was a huge hit.

During the sing-along Hart was standing in his favorite concert spot—the back row of the chorus. The kids had wanted him to be like the director and stand out front during the songs. He had refused. There was enough to worry about without having to look stupid and pretend he knew how to direct a chorus.

The words to "Jingle Bells" were coming out

of his mouth, but Hart's mind was flopping all over the place, whispering to itself, trying to remember a hundred things at once. *So . . . so next comes the Shalom song. How's the tune go? How's it go? Oh yeah, oh yeah . . . Then the dreidel stuff . . . .and it's a round . . . my group first, and then Billy's—or is his first? Wait . . . No . . . Shalom is the round . . . Which . . . and the batteries? Did Dad get 'em? 'Cause fifty's not enough . . . and the lights . . . 'cause that means . . . or does the dreidel song come next?*

As muddled as it was inside Hart's head, out in the hall behind the stage it was worse. The two kids inside the big dreidel costumes had been practicing their spinning, and one of them had just spread a good part of his dinner all over the floor. No one could find the custodian, and a mom and a dad were trying to manage the emergency cleanup with tissues and a bottle of spring water.

Colleen, the stage director, had three different little walkie-talkies clipped to the front of her sweater: one to talk to the kid running the spotlight, one for the kids moving props around the stage, and one to keep in touch with Mr. Meinert. She grabbed one of them and said, "Mr. Meinert, Mr. Meinert! One of the dreidels just threw up! Play an extra verse of 'Jingle Bells'!"

So the sing-along went on a little longer, and no one seemed to mind, especially Tim Miller.

Most of Hart's worries were unnecessary. *"Shalom Chevarim"* began as Jenna explained the connection between Hanukkah and the hope for peace. Hart loved this song. It had become his favorite during the rehearsals because the chorus sang it as a three part round. There was such a simple dignity to the melody all by itself, but by the time Hart joined in singing with the third group, the full effect of the harmony and the inter-woven strains was so beautiful, so powerful and real.

Up onstage, facing the audience filled with his family and his neighbors, Hart was glad to be in the back row when they sang *"Shalom Chevarim."* And he was glad there were so many other kids singing, because he felt his throat begin to tighten up. The music, the har-mony, the way the whole concert was flowing along—it all filled his heart in a way he'd never felt before.

Then "I Have a Little Dreidel" celebrated the lighter side of Hanukkah, and the big spinning dreidels got everyone laughing—except one small child in the front row who announced for all to hear, "Something smells like spit-up!"

After the dreidels took their bows, all of the students in the chorus walked off the stage single file, half down one side of the gym, half down the other. When they had surrounded the audience, each about four feet from the next, the lights dimmed a little and Mr. Meinert hit one soft chord on the piano. With no introduction, the chorus began to sing.

"O little town of Bethlehem,
How still we see thee lie.
Above thy deep and dreamless sleep,
The silent stars go by.
Yet in thy dark streets shineth
The everlasting light.
The hopes and fears of all the years
Are met in thee tonight."

Then the spotlight came up on Allie Marston. She read from a single sheet of paper.

"What are 'the hopes and fears of all the years?' Maybe the hope is our hope for peace. And maybe the fear is the fear that real peace will never come to the Earth. When the angels came to the shepherds near Bethlehem, they sang, 'On Earth, Peace, goodwill toward men.'

"This year, right now, that is our hope, and we share it with you."

The room went completely dark. Mr. Meinert played a short introduction on the piano, and at the front of the gym one girl turned on a flashlight and aimed it at her own face. It was Janie Kingston, and she sang the first two lines alone, her voice high and sweet. As more and more children joined the singing, each one lit a light.

"Let there be peace on earth,
And let it begin with me;
Let there be peace on earth,
The peace that was meant to be.

"With God our Creator,
Children all are we,
Let us walk with each other
In perfect harmony."

The piano played through the melody of the first two verses again, and seventy flashlight beams turned upward and met in the center, high above the audience. And into that brightness—with wings of gold and a silver gown—an angel descended.

It wasn't Lisa Morton. It was a doll she and her mom had made. Lisa's dad and big brother were up in the bleachers controlling it with a system of pulleys and fishing line.

As the angel began to fly a slow, graceful circle above the audience, all the flashlight beams followed it, and the singing resumed.

"Let peace begin with me,
Let this be the moment now;
With every step I take
Let this be my solemn vow:

"To take each moment
and live each moment

In peace eternally.
Let there be peace on earth
And let it begin with me."

The chorus repeated the last two lines, and
when it got to the words *with me*, Janie sang
them alone, and then ten other kids on the
other side of the audience repeated, "with
me," and then ten more sang it again, and it
went on through six repetitions until the
whole chorus sang the words one last time.
"With me!"

The lights came up, the chorus took a bow,
and then the entire audience—every mom and
dad, every grandmother and grandfather, aunt,
uncle, neighbor, and friend—they all jumped
to their feet and began to applaud. The
applause went on for one minute, and then
two, not wildly, not with hooting and stomp-
ing, but with deep feeling, and plenty of dab-
bing at the corners of the eyes.

The applause went on because all the people
knew they had just seen something extraordi-
nary, and because they all knew that if they
stopped clapping, the concert would be over.
And no one wanted it to end.

Mr. Meinert did not want it to end either.

He sat on the bench behind the piano. He did not stand, and he took no bow. But he did look out and catch his wife's eye as she stood there in the fourth row, tears running down her cheeks. He smiled, and so did she. And he knew that now Lucy Meinert understood. She understood why he hadn't quit, and why he would always believe that there's a future in teaching.

The applause finally stopped.

Hart Evans found his parents and endured a big hug from his mom. His sister Sarah made a face as she handed him a copy of the program. "Why does it say 'Sixth Grade Chorus, Hart Evans, Director'?"

Hart shrugged. "Probably a joke." But he carefully folded the program and put it in his back pocket.

His dad grabbed Hart's hand and shook it. "That was the *best* concert I have ever seen! 'Hart Evans, Director'—it's no joke. I am *very* proud of you."

Hart smiled, but he didn't know what to say, and he felt his face getting red. His dad came to the rescue.

"What do you say we all go out for some ice cream?"

Hart said, "Yeah, great." Then he turned quickly, looking for Mr. Meinert. He couldn't spot him. "Listen, I've got to go backstage for a second. Be right back."

Mr. Meinert wasn't on the stage or in the hallway behind it. Hart saw Colleen, and trotted over to her. "Colleen, nice job!"

Colleen smiled and said, "Thanks. You too."

"You seen Mr. Meinert?"

Colleen pointed. "He went that way with a stack of music. Probably going back to the music room."

Hart took off down the hallway.

twenty-one

CODA

When Hart peeked in the doorway of the music room, only one row of lights was on, down at the front of the room. Mr. Meinert was standing at his desk, staring into a cardboard file box.

Hart paused. It was something about the way the guy stood there, leaning slightly forward, both hands on the back of his chair. Hart felt like he was interrupting.

He knocked on the door frame anyway.

Mr. Meinert jumped a little, but when he saw it was Hart, his face broke into a big smile.

"Mr. Meinert? Can I come in?"

"Sure," he said. "What a *great* concert, Hart. Really. One of the best ever, anywhere."

Hart smiled back. "Thanks. I looked for you over in the gym, but you'd already left. And Colleen said you might be here. Because I just wanted to thank you. 'Cause if it hadn't been for you, we'd have never had a concert—I mean, not like this one." Hart suddenly felt embarrassed, felt another blush coming on. "So anyway . . . thanks." Hart walked to the desk and held out his right hand, and Mr. Meinert reached over and shook it.

And that's when Hart saw what was in the file box. A pair of orange-handled scissors with *D. Meinert* written on them. Mr. Meinert's "Great Musicians" desk calendar. A stack of *Music Educator* magazines, and six or seven books, each of them with *D. Meinert* scrawled on the cover.

"How come you're emptying your desk? You moving to a different room?"

Mr. Meinert paused. "I won't be back after the vacation. It's because of the budget cuts in the town. So I'm going to find work somewhere else."

Hart was stunned. "You mean they *fired* you? They can't do that! Who's going to teach chorus?"

Mr. Meinert smiled and held up a hand like a crossing guard. "No, no, no—not fired. They eliminated my job, and they *can* do that. And I don't know who's going to teach chorus. Or even if there'll be a chorus at all come January."

"But—but why didn't you tell everybody? We—we could have done something—like send letters . . . or make a petition . . . or start a big protest . . . *something*!"

Mr. Meinert smiled again. "That's *exactly* why the affected teachers asked that this be kept quiet until the vacation. We all had work to do, and we didn't want a lot of pity and worry from everybody else getting in the way."

Hart was stumped, almost angry. "But . . . but . . . it's not fair!"

Mr. Meinert nodded. "Couldn't agree more. But that's the way it is, for the moment anyway. Things can change. You know that. Things can change in all sorts of unexpected ways."

It was Mr. Meinert's turn to hold out his hand. "So this is good-bye, at least for now. It's been a pleasure working with you, Hart."

Hart shook his teacher's hand again, fighting back a lump in his throat. He managed a smile and said, "So long." And he turned and headed for the door.

"Hart—hold it a second. I want you to have this."

Hart walked back, and Mr. Meinert reached into his file box and pulled out an envelope. "I guess I can afford to give this up—I've still got another one."

He fished around in the envelope and then handed Hart a slightly used Number 16 rubber band.

Mr. Meinert reached into the envelope again and held up the other rubber band. "I probably shouldn't be saying this, but I'm going to anyway: Thanks for letting me have this. Turns out it was just what I needed."

Hart grinned. "Yeah," he said. "Worked out okay for me, too."

Mr. Meinert grabbed the box off his desk. "I've got to run. My wife's waiting out in the car. Listen, you have a happy holiday, Hart."

Hart nodded. "Yup. You too. See you around town, Mr. Meinert."

The teacher smiled. "You can count on it."

And as he followed Hart out of the music room, Mr. Meinert turned off the lights.

Andrew Clements is the author of more than forty books for children, including *Frindle*, *The Report Card*, and most recently *We the Children*, the first book in the Benjamin Pratt & the Keepers of the School series. He lives with his family outside Boston, Massachusetts.

Mr. Clements says of *The Last Holiday Concert*: "I knew the basic plot of *The Last Holiday Concert* before I began. But I learned as I was writing that the story is really about the difference between popularity and leadership. It's also about the vital role that art and music teachers play in our public schools."